THE SEVENTH LINK

Recent Titles by Margaret Mayhew from Severn House

A FOREIGN FIELD
DRY BONES
I'LL BE SEEING YOU
THE LAST WOLF
THE LITTLE SHIP
OLD SOLDIERS NEVER DIE
OUR YANKS
THE PATHFINDER
QUADRILLE
ROSEBUDS
THOSE IN PERIL
THREE SILENT THINGS
THE SEVENTH LINK

THE SEVENTH LINK

A Village Mystery

Margaret Mayhew

This first world edition published 2014
in Great Britain and the USA by
SEVERN HOUSE PUBLISHERS LTD of
19 Cedar Road, Sutton, Surrey, England, SM2 5DA.

Trade paperback edition published
in Great Britain and the USA 2015 by
SEVERN HOUSE PUBLISHERS LTD

British Library Cataloguing in Publication Data

Mayhew, Margaret, 1936- author.
  The Seventh Link.
  1. Reunions–Fiction. 2. Country life–Fiction.
  3. Detective and mystery stories.
  I. Title
  823.9'14-dc23

ISBN-13: 978-0-7278-8421-3 (cased)
ISBN-13: 978-1-84751-531-5 (trade paper)

Except where actual historical events and characters are being
described for the storyline of this novel, all situations in this
publication are fictitious and any resemblance to living persons
is purely coincidental.

All Severn House titles are printed on acid-free paper.

Severn House Publishers support the Forest Stewardship Council™ [FSC™],
the leading international forest certification organisation. All our titles that
are printed on FSC certified paper carry the FSC logo.

Typeset by Palimpsest Book Production Ltd.,
Falkirk, Stirlingshire, Scotland.
Printed and bound in Great Britain by
TJ International, Padstow, Cornwall.

For Lydia

AUTHOR'S NOTE

As readers will be aware, after many years' delay a magnificent memorial, paid for from public funds, has been erected in Green Park, London, standing as fitting tribute to the 55,573 young men of Bomber Command who gave their lives in the Second World War. At its heart are seven bronze sculptures depicting an air crew just returned from a bombing mission.

Unlike other services, no campaign medal was struck for Bomber Command at the end of the war and no official recognition or thanks given by the Government for their courageous contribution and self-sacrifice. Instead, they were pointedly ignored.

It was not until 2012 that the surviving veteran heroes of Bomber Command were finally awarded a clasp.

Freedom is the sure possession of those alone who have the courage to defend it

Pericles

The fighters are our salvation but the bombers alone provide the means of victory

Winston Churchill – 1940

ONE

Engine roaring, the Ford Escort shot backwards out of the driveway of the Cuthbertsons' bungalow, Shangri-La, narrowly missing the gate post. The Colonel, who happened to be walking across the village green on his way back from the Dog and Duck, glimpsed the Major's wife crouched over the wheel. Instead of her usual tweeds, Marjorie Cuthbertson was wearing a floral frock, probably dating from her Far Eastern memsahib days: a nod to the English summer and an unusual temperature in the upper seventies. The Escort jerked forward with a teeth-grating crash of gears and bounced off down the road, aimed in the direction of Dorchester. Today, he remembered, was the day for Mrs Cuthbertson's weekly visit to her hairdresser. It was also the day when she left a cold lunch out for her husband, which gave the Major the excuse to linger longer than usual at the Dog and Duck and air his views on life in general, and politicians in particular. The country was, naturally, going to the dogs. No standards, no decency, no respect, no pride, no backbone. Nothing but spongers and foreigners.

The Colonel had listened to many such diatribes in his time in bars all over the world. In fact, he didn't share that particular view, or at least, not about England. And it seemed to him that a great deal had improved in the country over the past fifty years or so. On the whole – both materially and physically – the people were far better off. They lived longer, travelled further, had more opportunities and fewer constraints. The children were benefiting most of all. They were better educated, healthier, taller, stronger, and the world was their oyster. As for the Major's foreigners, England had an old and very worthy tradition of welcoming, sheltering and absorbing people of all nationalities who, in return, contributed their talents and skills and colourful cultures.

He wasn't quite so sure about the spiritual side of things. Frog End's beautiful old Norman church was only half full on Sundays and not many people, himself included, believed in God any more. He had stopped believing when he had watched his wife, Laura, suffer and die horribly and now only went to church himself out of habit and an ingrained sense of duty, and because he liked singing the hymns. People worshipped other things now: celebrities, football, shopping, the latest gadgets, foreign holidays, TV soaps.

The Colonel had been compulsorily retired from the army, aged fifty-five and, in the same year his wife, Laura, had died. He had stayed on in their small flat in London for ten more years, trying his hand at a variety of jobs, including selling double-glazing, and he had discovered in the process that his thirty-seven years in the army counted for nothing in the outside world. Finally, he had sold the London flat and moved to a cottage in the village of Frog End in Dorset. The place had been in a bad state, neglected for years and full of faults, but the eager young estate agent who had showed him round had insisted that it had what he called potential. What had sold it to him, in spite of all the faults, had been the fact that it had been Laura's dream cottage. They had happened to notice it when they had been touring in the West Country while home on leave one summer. They had stopped at the Dog and Duck, sat on a bench outside and admired the mass of pink roses climbing over the walls of the thatched cottage on the other side of the green. From a distance and on a beautiful sunny day, it had looked charming and Laura had said it was just the sort of place she had always dreamed of living in one day. Years later, after her death, he had been staying with friends in that same part of the world and had driven round the countryside, revisiting some of the places they had seen together, in a vain attempt to recapture the past. He had found Frog End again and the thatched cottage, looking far less charming close up and in grey winter, had been for sale. It was called Pond Cottage and, against all common sense and reason, he had bought it.

He walked on towards the cottage, aware from a reflected glint at the sitting-room window of Lupin Cottage on the other side of the green that he was being tracked by Miss Butler with her German U-boat captain's binoculars. A former Wren, long-retired, she had acquired the Zeiss glasses on the death of her fearsome Admiral father. It was not quite certain how they had come into the possession of the Admiral himself since he had, apparently, only ever sailed a desk during the Second World War. Freda Butler, the Colonel knew, now used them to observe the village comings and goings. Unlike their original owner, though, she had no predatory intentions. She was merely curious.

The Colonel reached Pond Cottage and let himself in at the front door. He had grown more used to the emptiness and silence of living alone, though it had taken more than a year to make the adjustment. He was fortunate to have a good neighbour, Naomi Grimshaw, a widowed divorcee, who lived in Pear Tree Cottage next door, and he had gradually come to know most people in the village, at least by sight if not personally. And, of course, he had Thursday, the torn-eared black-and-tan stray who had turned up out of the blue on that particular day of the week and had consented, magnanimously, to stay.

The old cat was sound asleep on the sofa in the sitting room. When he woke up, he would stir and stretch before going to sit in the kitchen in front of his bowl and wait for a decent supper to be served. A box of dry cat food shaken over the bowl would not do. It must be some tempting gourmet feline offering, prepared by the makers, so it some-times seemed to the Colonel, with more care and thought than was often given to food for human consumption.

Afterwards, Thursday would take a stroll in the garden,

probably spending some time staring into the pond and watching the six small gold fish that the Colonel had bought from a pet shop. He had gone in to buy cat food, spotted them swimming desperately round and round in a very small glass bowl and taken pity on them. They seemed to like their spacious new home and the food he fed them. Thursday seemed to like them too and would watch them with very close attention. Occasionally, the Colonel took a tail count. If the six became five, or less, he would know whom to blame.

When he had first moved into the cottage, the garden had been a tangled wilderness of brambles and nettles with no sign of any pond. Under the direction of Naomi, an expert gardener, and with the services of the gardener/handyman Jacob who normally worked at the Manor in the village, the ground had gradually been cleared. Along with the reclaimed flower beds and some nice old trees and shrubs, the pond had gradually emerged into view from under a thick covering of brambles – weed-choked and silted up, but still a pond that had made sense of the cottage's name.

The Colonel went into the kitchen at the back of the cottage and made himself a sandwich of sliced ham from the fridge, with a generous smear of Coleman's English mustard and some lettuce. He took it out to his shed in the garden.

The shed was a recent acquisition and he was very pleased with its looks. A good, solid structure with no summer-house pretensions or any resemblance to Swiss chalets, as Naomi had feared. Flat roof, wood walls, two plain windows and one unglazed door. Best of all, it was a place where he would be left undisturbed. People often stopped by the cottage, asking for his help with some village matter. Manning a jumble sale stall, serving on a committee, collecting for a charity, and so on. He was usually happy to oblige, but he had recently been door-stepped by Mrs Bentley of the summer fête cake stall, with the aim of wheedling him into joining the Frog End Amateur Dramatic Society. Apparently, they were putting on a performance of Agatha Christie's play *The Mousetrap* and new blood was needed. He had stood his ground, for once. Not long ago he had been asked to give a lecture in the village hall about his life in the army. He had agreed, though reluctantly, and Major Cuthbertson who had lived in the village for far longer – had been greatly put out at not being asked instead. The slight still rankled.

More recently, the new vicar, Tony Morris, had called and stayed for some time. He had nothing against the well-meaning young man whom Naomi had written-off as the happy-clappy, guitar-playing type, and who unfortunately also had a beard, but he had no desire whatever to discuss God with him.

As it happened, the vicar had called to ask if he would agree to become a sidesman.

'Not too arduous, Colonel. It would only be for the second Sunday of every other month. You'd have various small duties to perform – taking off the altar cloth before the service, putting out the candlesticks, switching on the lectern light, greeting members of the congregation as they arrive, handing out hymn books and service sheets, and so on. Don't worry, you would be given full written instructions.'

It was little enough to ask, he thought.

'Yes, of course.'

'And I wonder if you'd consider your name going on the rota to read the lesson at matins? If you'll forgive me for a personal remark, you have a very good voice. Just the sort that people would find easy to listen to and understand.'

Again, he agreed but more reluctantly. He would be reading things he didn't believe in, which seemed quite wrong. But was it really any worse than singing hymns with words he didn't believe in either?

The conversation had moved on to a bold new project to make the pews in the parish church movable. The aim, the vicar had explained, was to provide open space so that the church was more welcoming to the young generation.

'They find it forbidding as it is.'

'Really?' He had thought that rather unlikely. Gnarled old pews like the ones in St Luke's were friendly things. You could sit in them, loll around in them, go to sleep in them during long sermons, if you so wished – and people had been doing so for many, many years.

'We need to be free of the constraints of fixed pews, Colonel. And, personally, I think churches look a lot better without them cluttering up the nave. Stacking chairs are a very viable option. A certain percentage of pews could be remade and the rest would be dismantled and their historic wood put to other good uses. For instance, we need to make the church accessible to those with disabilities and to eliminate any trip hazards.'

The Colonel was all for helping the disabled in every possible way, but he could not quite see how remaking some of the pews and chopping up the others was necessarily going to achieve it.

The vicar, who had been wearing socks and sandals, which would not have improved his standing with Naomi, had continued enthusiastically. 'And it would reduce our carbon footprint.'

'How so?'

'We have to keep our heating costs down and we have had expert advice that the most efficient way would be an underfloor system. But it would be impossible with the existing fixed pews and flooring.'

'You mean the old flagstones would have to go as well?'

'A smooth flat surface would be much more practical – say, of Purbeck stone.'

'No trip hazards?'

'Exactly. And we have to remember, Colonel, that for several hundred years, churches had no fixed pews at all. The nobs had movable seating but the ordinary folk stood or knelt on cold stone. Of course, a public meeting will be held so that all parishioners can air their views freely. There are bound to be some objections, but I'm confident that the majority will support the project.'

The Colonel had had no doubt that there would be plenty of very robust objections but he had kept his own reservations to himself. He was a new boy, after all, as well as a non-believer. Token appearances at matins, going through the motions with prayers, singing the hymns, even reading the lesson, did not entitle him to voice opinions about doing away with nice old pews and ancient flagstones. The conversation had petered out eventually, with only a brief reference to God, and the Colonel had seen the vicar out.

Now he unlocked the door of his new and secure retreat and surveyed it with quiet satisfaction. He had never possessed such a thing before. An impregnable bolt-hole from the world where he could do exactly as he pleased, without comment or interference or interruption from anyone, even Naomi. In fact, especially Naomi, whose attempts to get in had been thwarted but who had been known to peer in through the window if given half a chance. Which was why he had rigged up sacking curtains to be deployed whenever necessary and why he always kept the door locked.

Everything was in order and in its place. Nails and screws and nuts and bolts all neatly sorted into separate jars on the shelves. He had bought a proper work bench with a vice at one end and a compartment designed to take tools – hammer, chisel, wrenches, files and screwdrivers so that he could put his hand straight on whichever was needed. The garden tools – spade, forks, shears, trowel – were hanging on another wall, the lawn mower kept in a corner out of the way.

At first, he had used the workbench for doing general repairs – mending a wonky kitchen chair, gluing the china bowl he had broken, replacing the missing beading on the table that stood beside his fireside chair. Serious carpentry

– creating something from scratch – he rather feared beyond his capabilities, though he planned to give it a go one day. The idea of making a model of some kind had come to him when he had been lying awake one night and in the morning he had gone to the model shop in Dorchester and come out with a 1/35th scale kit of a Matilda Infantry Tank, glue, paint and brushes. A modest beginning. There had been kits for other famous tanks: the Russian T-34, the German Panzer, the American Sherman, the Chinese Norinco . . . but, in the end, he had settled for the British Matilda: the Battle Maiden of the Second World War. There was a Mark 11 kept in the Bovington Tank Museum, near Dorchester which he and his small grandson, Eric, had admired on their visit there together. Though the Colonel had not served in a tank regiment himself, he had always had the greatest respect for the brave men who had fought in one, risking a horrible death. The Germans had gruesomely called them Tommy Cookers.

He put the sandwich down at the edge of the bench. There was a picture of the tank on the lid of the kit box and, like the one in the museum, the Matilda was painted in a strange camouflage configuration. The intention, he had discovered, was not invisibility but to make the tank look like something else, facing a different way. Heavily armoured and impervious to most enemy anti-tank weapons of the time, rotating turret armed with a two-pounder and ninety-three armour-piercing rounds, as well as a Besa machine gun and smoke grenades, the Battle Maiden, Matilda had proved her worth in the mud of Europe, the sands of North Africa, the jungles of the Pacific and the snows of Russia. Her heavy armour plating slowed her down but, on the other hand, she crossed trenches and difficult terrain with ease. Her only fault, it seemed, was a somewhat unreliable steering mechanism.

The Colonel opened the box and unfolded the instruction leaflet. It was written in twelve different languages and he studied the English section for a moment. Diagrams showed the steps to follow and every part had a number. The plastic parts were sealed in a bag and moulded on to trees, to be cut off in turn and sanded smooth. The trick, apparently, was to get the sub-assemblies glued together first. He started with Step One and the wheel units.

TWO

The fiddly task absorbed him so completely that he was oblivious to time passing and he was about to move on to Step Five – fitting the track around the main gears and wheels – when there was a tapping at the shed window. He looked up to see Naomi's face peering at him through the glass. She was brandishing something that looked like a jar of jam. When he glanced at his watch he saw that it was well past six, which accounted for Naomi's arrival, with or without the jam.

He abandoned the tank track, tugged the sacking across the windows and went to unlock the door. Naomi, he knew, would be there in a flash but he had become adept at exiting and closing the door behind him in one quick movement so that she had no time to see inside. He was already relocking the door when she came round the corner.

'There you are, Hugh!'

He smiled at her as he dropped the key into his pocket. 'Yes, indeed, Naomi. Here I am.'

Like the Major's wife, her customary clothing had changed radically with the hot weather. Instead of a tracksuit, she was wearing some kind of flowing ankle-length purple garment with a gentleman's broad-brimmed panama hat on her head. However, she still wore her white moon-boot trainers on her feet.

'I've brought you some of my raspberry jam.' She waved the pot at him. 'My own raspberries.'

'That's very kind of you, Naomi.'

It was. And he appreciated all the neighbourly kindnesses that she had shown him since he had moved in: help and advice with taming the wilderness he had taken on for a garden, simple recipes for simple meals that he had learned to cook for himself, chicken soup when he had gone down with a bad bout of flu, pears from her pear tree, plum jam from her Victoria plum tree, jars of home-made chutney. And gossip. She knew about everything that went on in the village and he rather enjoyed listening to her talk because the gossip was never malicious. She merely reported. It was extraordinary, he discovered, what went on beneath the surface of what appeared to be a totally stagnant pond.

He took the pot of jam from her. 'Thank you so much.'

There was a label stuck crookedly on the front and Naomi had scrawled on it in green biro: *Rasberry Jam.* She was a wonderful gardener and an excellent cook, but hopeless at spelling. The jam, he knew, would be delicious however its name was spelled.

'Would you like a drink?'

'I thought you'd never ask.'

He always did, though. Naomi was particularly fond of his Chivas Regal whisky and they had drunk many a glass together beside his sitting-room fire in winter and now, in summer, out on the flagstone terrace at the back of Pond Cottage which she had encouraged him to have built. He wondered, sometimes, if her motive had been entirely altruistic.

He went indoors to fetch the drinks. Thursday was sitting in front of his bowl in the kitchen, waiting with feigned indifference for his supper to be served. Unlike dogs, cats never lowered themselves to beg or grovel. The Colonel served up tinned sardines, mashing them up in consideration of the old cat's missing teeth. Then he went into the sitting room where the whisky decanter was kept on the sideboard and carried it out on a tray with glasses and a jug of water.

Naomi was already sitting in one of the chairs on the terrace, waiting for service like Thursday, but without the feigned indifference. He added the required splash of water to her glass and sat down with his own. No water for him – he took it straight – and no ice for either of them. Ice, in Naomi's opinion was a complete waste of space and, as far as he was concerned, it got in the way of tasting a good whisky. Naomi seized her glass.

'Cheers, Hugh. Down the hatch.'

'Cheers.'

'Aaaah . . . that's better.'

'Bad day?'

She fanned herself with the panama hat. 'Can't stand this heat. It's as ghastly as Australia.'

Naomi's only son and his family lived in Brisbane and her one visit out there had not been a great success.

He said, 'Well, you're looking remarkably cool in that very nice gown.'

'It's not a gown, it's a kaftan.'

'Don't tell me you bought it in Dorchester?'

'Good lord, no! I found it in the trunk in the attic. Belonged to my mother. She got it in Turkey years and years ago.'

The trunk in Naomi's attic had already yielded up a number of gems from the past – a wolfskin hat of possible Cossack origin, her grandfather's Canadian lumberjack's cap, a magnificent Edwardian flower, feather and straw creation belonging to her Great Aunt Rosalind – and now the exotic Turkish kaftan.

'What about the panama?' He'd had one himself once though God only knew where it was now. Maybe up in his own attic?

'My father's.' She tweaked the wavy brim. 'It was near the bottom so it'd got a bit squashed. Jolly useful in this weather. Keeps the sun off.' She slapped it back on her head and tilted it forward over her eyes. 'Garden's looking good, Hugh.'

She was being kind again. Personally, he thought it was

looking rather dusty and tired. The August heat was taking a toll; the colours fading, the green not nearly so fresh.

He said, 'The delphiniums have been a bit of a disaster.'

The deep blue ones he had planted with such high hopes towards the back of the border had been beaten down by a spell of heavy rain in July and seemed to have given up altogether.

'They can be tricky. You've got to stake them properly or they'll keel over.'

'I think I might take them out and get something else.'

She wagged a finger at him. 'Give them a chance, Hugh. Nature can't be rushed. I'm all in favour of getting rid of total failures but you'd be surprised how some plants rally. Did you talk to them?'

He had, in fact, admonished them rather than delivering the sort of encouraging pep talk that Naomi had in mind.

'Not exactly.'

'You must, Hugh. It works wonders. People always think Prince Charles is crackers to talk to his plants but it's perfectly sane. I see you cut the white lavenders.'

'Yes, I remembered.'

Eight, eight, eight was the golden rule that she had drummed into him: cut them on the eighth day of the eighth month down to eight inches and in a hedgehog shape. He had done so dutifully but doubtfully.

'They're looking a bit shocked, don't you think?'

'They'll get over it. You don't want them going all leggy on you, do you?'

'If you say so, Naomi.'

'I do. Lavenders need a firm hand. The Veronicas are doing well.'

'They don't seem to give any trouble.'

'They must like being where you put them. The right plant in the right place – that's the secret. I gave a talk on that subject for Ruth at the Manor the other day. It went down rather well.'

Ruth had inherited Frog End Manor when her late mother, the unpopular Lady Swynford, had died last summer. She had, in fact, done more than just die. She had been murdered during the village fête. Smothered with a pillow upstairs in her bedroom at the Manor while the brass band played on merrily in the garden below – possibly during their spirited rendition of 'The Dambusters March'. There had been a police investigation but the Colonel had made his own deductions. In the end, the murderer had confessed.[1]

Ruth had since married the nice young local doctor, Tom Harvey, and the Colonel had been very touched to have been asked to give her away at the wedding. Ruth had given up her job in London and started a small business growing and selling plants at the Manor, which was proving a real success. He had bought a number of plants there and found it a very satisfying experience. Few garden centres seemed to have staff who knew anything about their bought-in plants, whereas Ruth could tell you all about hers because she had raised them from scratch. She knew which ones would suit his garden, where to plant them, how much water to give, when to prune, and so on, and she grew unusual varieties that he had never heard of. From time to time Naomi gave a talk at the Manor, booming out instructions and golden rules while drawing big diagrams with shrieking chalk on a blackboard. The talks were always packed out.

'Well, I'm very sorry I missed it.'

'Forgot to tell you about it. Sonia Finsbury's giving one on peonies and irises the week after next.'

He wasn't sure about the peonies but the irises were certainly a draw.

'That sounds interesting.'

'She knows her onions.'

'I'm sure.' He had seen Mrs Finsbury in action on the Village Hall Committee.

---

[1] See *Old Soldiers Never Die*

Naomi took a swig of her whisky. 'By the way, I think Ruth might be in the family way already.'

'Oh. What makes you think that?'

'Her eyes. You can often tell from women's eyes. They look funny. I'll keep you posted.'

He had no doubt that she would. Not much would escape Naomi, or anyone else in Frog End. There was village surveillance network that put the Russian KGB to shame.

Naomi said, 'Did you hear about our happy-clappy vicar's latest brainwave?'

He said cautiously, 'Which one?'

'Not content with trying to foist that ghastly modern church-speak on us, twanging his guitar and wanting everyone to make signs of peace to each other, he's now cooked up some lunatic scheme of getting rid of the old pews and having stacking chairs instead. The man's an idiot! Does he really think the Diocesan lot would allow it?'

'It seems unlikely, I agree.'

'There's to be a public meeting so that everyone can say what they think and they won't mince their words. He'll be shot down in flames.'

She hadn't mentioned the underfloor heating or the Purbeck stone and he felt it was wiser not to either.

Fortunately, Naomi was off on another tack.

'You should get a proper greenhouse, Hugh. Much more use to you than a shed. Can't think why you spend so much time shut up in there. What on earth do you do?'

He had no intention of satisfying her curiosity. 'I like it in there, Naomi.'

'Well, I'll never understand men and their sheds. Cecil was just the same.'

Cecil was Naomi's late and unlamented former husband. He had gone off with his secretary and then died, leaving Naomi a widowed divorcee – if such a thing were possible. In any case, Naomi always described herself as a widow *tout court* which, she said, had a far better image. The widowed were always viewed with sympathy and respect.

Thursday had finished his sardine supper and walked across the terrace towards the lawn. He ignored them completely. Naomi, who frequently ejected him from his winter spot on the end of the sofa closest to the fire, did not meet with his approval. Also, Naomi was a dog person and she had two Jack Russell terriers, Mutt and Jeff to prove it. Not that *they* had ever given Thursday any trouble, having too much respect for his sharp claws.

Naomi said, 'Thursday's beginning to show his age a bit. Whatever it is.'

The Colonel had no idea what it was. Somewhere approximating to his own age in cat years, he imagined. Or perhaps more. He watched the cat making his way across the lawn – a little stiffly perhaps, but that was all.

'Do you think so? I hadn't noticed.'

'Don't worry, Hugh. He'll go on for years. Cats like him don't give up easily.'

He remembered the time when Thursday had gone missing while he had been away and he had feared the worst. Naomi had come round to feed him in his absence but Thursday had demonstrated his disapproval of the arrangement by going away too. In the end, he had come back, but it had been a worrying few days.[2]

He said, 'Perhaps I ought to take him to a vet for a check-up?'

'Has he ever been put in a cat basket?'

'Not as far as I know.'

'Well, I doubt if he'd take kindly to it, or to the vet either.'

'No . . . probably not such a good idea.'

Thursday had reached the pond and sat down at the edge to gaze into its depths. The attraction, of course, was the

---

[2] See *Dry Bones*

goldfish – unless he was admiring his reflection in the water which seemed unlikely, given his battle-scarred looks.

He said, 'Actually, I've been meaning to ask you, Naomi, whether you know of a good cattery – somewhere where I could leave Thursday for a few days? An old friend has asked me to visit and I'd rather like to go if I can.'

'I'll always feed him for you.'

'That's very kind of you, Naomi, but you know what he's like. He'd almost certainly go off again, like the last time. The only safe thing to do is to lock him up in a cattery – if I can find a good one.'

'He'll hate it. I put Mutt and Jeff into kennels when I went to Australia and they were miserable.'

'It would only be for a few days.'

'Well, I met some woman the other day at the WI who runs a cattery just outside Dorchester. She was dotty about cats. Has five of her own as well as the paying guests. You could go and take a look. See what it's like.'

'What was her name?'

'I can't remember, but the place was called "Cat Heaven". I laughed when she told me, then I realized that she was perfectly serious.'

'I'll look it up in the Yellow Pages.'

'Where does your friend live?'

'Lincolnshire.'

'Bomber county,' Naomi said. 'That's all I know about it. Masses of RAF bomber stations during the war, weren't there? An uncle of mine was a pilot and I remember he was stationed in Lincs. Awfully nice chap. He used to come and stay with us sometimes when he was on leave and tell us gory stories. He was one of the lucky ones to survive.'

'A lot of them didn't.'

The casualty figures were shocking. Of all the British armed services, Bomber Command had come off worst. He admired the men who had fought entombed in tanks during the Second World War, but the bomber crews had faced an equally horrible end up in the skies.

'Is your old friend anything to do with the RAF?'

'No, nothing.'

'Army?'

'Not that either. He worked for one of the big banks, but he's retired now.'

He and Laura had come across the Cheethams while they had been in Singapore. They had met at the Tanglin Club, played bridge and tennis together and become good friends. When the Cheethams had gone back to England they had kept in touch. Then Laura had died and Anne had been killed in a car accident and, two years ago, Geoffrey had remarried and moved up to Lincolnshire.

He said, 'I've never met his wife. His first one died. It's a second marriage.'

'Always a risky step.'

Unlike himself, Naomi took a jaundiced view of marriage.

'It's been rather a success, so far as I know. They run a Bed and Breakfast.'

'I can't imagine anything worse. Strangers in your home, sleeping in your beds. Having to cook those awful English breakfasts that the English never actually eat. What do *you* have for breakfast, Hugh?'

'Usually a piece of toast and a cup of coffee.'

'Same here. Except mine's tea.'

'Well, they seem to be doing very well.'

Geoffrey had sounded hale and hearty when he had phoned, as though his new life was suiting him. The house in Lincolnshire had been his new wife's childhood home and they had taken it on when her parents had died. Heather, he had gathered, was considerably younger than Geoffrey and full of energy, which was probably just as well. The Colonel rather agreed with Naomi about running a B & B.

'When will you go?'

'They've asked me for the weekend after next. Apparently,

there's some kind of RAF Reunion going on that they thought I might find interesting.'

'It'll do you good, Hugh. Make a change. Let's face it, Frog End's not the most exciting place in the world.'

He smiled. 'I wouldn't say that, Naomi. There always seems to be plenty going on.'

Cat Heaven, he learned from the Yellow Pages, was situated on the other side of Dorchester. *Expert care and attention given by a lifetime lover of cats. Luxurious and spacious accommodation, heated throughout the colder months. Individual needs and preferences catered for and veterinary expertise always on hand if necessary.*

When he rang the number given, the woman who answered sounded calm and reassuring. He explained the problem and Thursday.

'I'm very used to cats requiring special care,' the voice told him. 'I take all sorts. Would you like to come and see Cat Heaven for yourself?'

He drove over to make the inspection. The cattery was at the rear of an unassuming house on the outskirts of Dorchester and there was a painted sign of a very happy-looking cat by the front gate. The owner, Mrs Moffat, was a middle-aged woman with a beehive of dyed blonde hair and wearing something akin to Naomi's kaftan, but in black. He followed her round the side of the house to the cat hotel that had been built in the back garden. He saw at once that this was five-star accommodation. Each cage had two floors with a connecting ramp. The lower level provided a cushioned chair and a view out and the upper floor had a door for peace and privacy as well as a basket furnished with a heating pad. The view featured a well-stocked bird table providing a constant cabaret for the guests. And it was all spotlessly clean.

'I encourage my owners to bring their cats' own blankets and toys,' Mrs Moffat told him. 'It helps them to feel at home.'

Thursday had no such things and the Colonel had never thought to provide them. He had a feeling that, in any case, they would have been summarily rejected or ignored. Strays had no use for pointless props; only for food and shelter.

'I'm afraid he may not take kindly to being locked up,' he said. 'I doubt if it's ever happened to him before. He's very much his own cat, if you understand me.'

She nodded vigorously. 'I understand perfectly, Colonel. I'm used to dealing with all sorts. I find that they usually trust me. Cats always know if people are cat people. It's instinctive.'

He thought of Thursday giving Naomi a wide berth, and of the different receptions accorded to visitors to the cottage – villagers, electricians, repair men, window cleaners, Jacob the gardener. Thursday always sorted them out.

He was taken on an inspection, proceeding down the row of cages. They contained a wide variety of cats from aristocratic pedigrees to humble moggies. Some were curled up quietly, others – usually the oriental ones – yowled and clawed at the mesh as they went by. All of them seemed well-cared-for and reasonably happy – as much as a prisoner, human or animal, could ever be.

He booked Thursday into Cat Heaven and learned that an inoculation was required from the vet before he could be accepted. On his way home, he stopped at the pet shop and bought a cat carrier.

The question was how to get Thursday inside it? The Colonel had never committed the lese-majesty of trying to pick him up, any more than Thursday had ever attempted to sit on his lap. Their relationship had been conducted on a strictly formal level – their evenings spent with the Colonel in his wing chair and the cat at the fireside end of the sofa, plus the occasional stroll together in the garden with Thursday following at a studiedly non-committal distance.

Surprise was the only way. In his time in the army, the Colonel had learned that surprise was always the key to a successful attack. You had to catch your objective off-guard. He made an appointment with the vet and when Thursday was curled up asleep on the sofa he scooped him up from over the sofa's back in a lightning movement, inserted him straight into the carrier and slammed the door.

On the car journey, Thursday glared balefully through the grille and then hissed and spat at everyone and everything in the waiting room. The vet, a cheerful young man in khaki shorts, didn't attempt to coax him out but simply tipped the carrier on end so that he slithered, scrabbling wildly, on to the table. On the whole, the vet said, giving Thursday a rapid examination after the injection, the old cat was in pretty good shape considering his former lifestyle and his age which was probably somewhere around fifteen. He had a few teeth missing and a touch of arthritis in the hind legs but the rest of him seemed all right. The torn ear wasn't worth trying to repair.

The Colonel's daughter, Alison, rang that evening.

'How are you, Dad?'

'Fine.'

Unlike his daughter-in-law, Susan, she never tried to interfere in his life. Her own was extremely busy and successful and he was proud of it, though he sometimes wished that she would find a good man to share it with her. The high-powered job was all very well but it shouldn't be everything.

He told her about the visit to the vet, which made her laugh.

'I bet Thursday was furious.'

'It had to be done. I'm putting him in a cattery while I go away for a few days. He needed a clean bill of health.'

'Are you going somewhere nice?'

'Lincolnshire. Someone your mother and I knew out in Singapore. His first wife died and he's remarried.'

'I wish you'd do the same, Dad. You must get pretty lonely on your own in the country.'

'It can be just as lonely in a town.'

'Aren't there any nice widows down there?'

'I've got one next door.'

'Naomi's not what I meant.'

There were, indeed, several widows in the village. He'd met them all and, pleasant as they were, he couldn't imagine living with any of them.

He changed the subject. 'When are you coming to stay?'

'Well, I have to go to a meeting in New York next week and I thought I'd go and visit some people I know over there. They've got a place in Martha's Vineyard. It'll probably be September before I can get down. Is Marcus bringing Susan and the children to see you?'

'They rather want me to go to them instead.'

The thought of doing so had depressed him and he had prevaricated. The house in Norwich was pin-neat and highly polished. Susan would make him eat healthy, meatless food, there would be no whisky in the evenings and no wine either and he would be forced to go and view any bungalows up for sale in the area with the object of him moving in to one of them. True, there would be the compensation of spending time with his grandson, Eric, and of getting to know his new granddaughter, Edith, but he would have preferred to do so on his own territory and on his own terms.

The bond he had forged with Eric – a spoiled brat if ever there was one – had come about when the child had stayed at Pond Cottage with him while Susan had been in hospital with a threatened miscarriage. The Colonel had taken him to the Tank Museum at Bovington nearby where Eric had stopped being spoiled and been spellbound instead. He had regaled his grandson with tank facts and figures, pulling no punches with the gory details. They had rounded off their visit with a canteen lunch of chicken nuggets, baked beans, chips and lurid pink ice cream – all the sort of things that Susan forbade at home.

Alison said, 'Can't you persuade them to come to you?'

'Susan's not very keen on travelling with the baby.'

'That's pathetic.'

Alison, he knew, had very little patience with her sister-in-law, and nothing at all in common with her, which was a shame. She and Marcus had once been close but, inevitably and rightly, Marcus's first loyalties now lay with his wife and family.

They talked for a bit longer and then she rang off. He lifted the phone receiver again. Susan would have to be rung. He had promised to let her know if he went away. On the last occasion, when he had failed to do so, she had been on the point of phoning the police by the time he had returned. He dialled the number and his daughter-in-law answered. There was the usual exchange about his health and his diet and he gave the usual lies. No, he wasn't eating any fatty things or junk foods. Yes, he was taking the vitamin pills she had given him, yes, he was eating a lot of pasta which she always insisted was so good for him and which he thoroughly disliked.

'When are you going to come up and stay with us, Father?'

If only she would call him Hugh!

'Wouldn't that be too much trouble for you?'

'No, Edith is sleeping through now. And Eric keeps asking about you. He'd like to see you soon.'

He felt very guilty. 'I'd like to see him too. If you came down here, I could take him to the tank museum again. I think he'd enjoy that.'

'I really don't feel I could face the journey, Father – not with all the baby things. There'd be such a lot to bring and I need to keep Edith to her routine. That's very important.'

'Yes, of course. Well, I'll certainly come soon.'

'You remember that nice bungalow down the road I told you about that was for sale?'

He did, indeed. She had mentioned it a number of times. 'Yes?'

'Well, somebody was going to buy it but then the sale fell through so it's back on the market again. You really ought to go and view it when you come to stay, Father. I think you'd like it. It would be very easy to run. Much easier than your cottage with all those old beams and those dangerous stairs. And just a small garden all on one level with only a little bit of lawn. And it's got full gas central heating and parquet floors and the kitchen is brand new. It's even got a garbage disposal so you'd hardly have any rubbish to put out.'

He realized how decrepit he must seem to her: incapable of coping with stairs, rubbish, mowing or much else.

'Really? That sounds interesting. By the way, Susan, I was ringing to tell you that I'm going to be away for a few days.'

'Oh?' Her tone sharpened, alert to any potential trouble. 'Where are you going?'

'Up to Lincolnshire. An old friend has moved there. He and his wife run a Bed and Breakfast.'

Her reaction matched Naomi's. 'Oh, I couldn't do that! Imagine having strangers in your home!'

'I won't be a stranger. Anyway, I just thought I'd let you know.'

'We worry about you, Father. That time we couldn't get hold of you was awful. We were sure something had happened to you. That you'd had an accident in the home or out in the garden and nobody would know. You could be lying there for days.'

He said drily, 'I think they'd find out soon enough.'

'But you'd be so much safer in a bungalow and living near us. And we wouldn't have to worry.'

He said gently but firmly: 'It's good of you to be so concerned, Susan, but there's really no need. I'm not yet senile and I can still look after myself perfectly well. And,' he added, equally firmly, 'As it happens, I don't care for bungalows at all.'

She was hurt, of course, and he was very sorry about it but there was only so much interference that he was prepared to tolerate, however well meant.

Later, he went out to the shed and resumed work on the Matilda tank. He was on Step Nine and it was taking shape quite nicely.

THREE

Geoffrey Cheetham was staring into the depths of the lake. Lake was a rather grand name for it, but it was big enough to be able to go for a decent row in the old dinghy and the B & B guests were welcome to take it out any time they liked. It could accommodate five quite comfortably, even more at a pinch. Most of them didn't bother, though.

The good thing about B & Bs, as he had discovered, was that the guests never stayed for long. Overnight, or maybe two nights, or even three, but not usually more than that. They moved on elsewhere or went back home. Also, they were not there during the day. In general, as he had also discovered, they were well-behaved, considerate, and anxious to please and be pleased. He and Heather had put up foreigners at The Grange from all over the world, as well as the home-grown British. Americans, Australians, Dutch, German, French, Italian, Swedes. On the whole, he favoured the Americans. They were always so impressed by everything – the old house, the oil paintings, the furnishings, the gardens, the lake.

The only problem about the lake was the blanket weed. He had fought a pitched battle, donning chest-high waders to get to close grips with the enemy, heaving himself through the thick mud bottom and tearing the weed out in handfuls, all to the point of exhaustion. Then he had read somewhere that pulling it out only made things worse as thousands more spores were released into the water. Three weeks ago he had tried some new stuff that claimed to clean up ponds within two weeks. The explanatory leaflet showed a photograph of goldfish swimming happily around in crystal-clear,

weedless water. He had followed the maker's instructions
to the letter, sprinkling the granules evenly over the surface
and he had taken the dinghy out to do more sprinkling where
it was too deep for his waders. So far, there had been no
difference and the only time he caught a glimpse of the fish
was when they came up to the surface when they saw *him*
through the weed. One or two of them were doing that now
– plopping up by the bank where he was standing in the
hope that he had brought them something to eat. But over-
feeding the fish was said to encourage the weed and make
it grow even faster, so he was careful not to do that any
more.

He had no idea how many fish there were in the lake but
some of them seemed to have grown quite large. The biggest
was a ghost carp that very occasionally appeared – silver-
white and two feet long at least, gliding by silently. Spooky,
he always felt. Come to think of it, there was something
rather sinister about all fish. The fact was they'd strip the
flesh from your bones if they got half the chance. You
weren't only the provider of food you *were* food, potentially
speaking. Hauling himself round in his waders, he never
felt comfortable if they came too near.

He walked back across the lawn towards the house where
Heather was still clearing breakfast things away in the
kitchen. He had already done his bit earlier in the day,
waiting at the table in the dining room, carrying in tea or
coffee, the plates of full English breakfasts, the racks of
toast. Making polite conversation to guests as he did so.
Had they slept well? Had they got everything they needed?
Would they like more toast? More milk? More coffee? More
tea? He knew all the stock questions and the answers were
nearly always the same. Yes, they had slept very well, thank
you. Yes, they had everything, thank you. No, they wouldn't
be needing any more toast. Or any more, milk, coffee, or
tea either. It was all perfect, thank you very much.

At the moment they only had one guest. Some wacko

woman who was taking part in the Tudor re-enactment they did every summer up at the Hall. They dressed up in period costume, spoke in olde English and pretended to be Tudor cooks, or labourers, or seamstresses or mummers, or whatever. He'd no objection to the concept – each to his or her own – but he thought it was carrying things too far to come down to breakfast already in costume and insist on conversing in olde English – which was what was happening every morning with Miss Warner. He'd had more than enough of the forsooths and by-your-leaves, the methinks and prithees while he was trying to serve her breakfast, and, unlike most guests, she was staying for what seemed to him to be an interminable length of time.

This evening seven more guests were due to arrive. Eight, if he included, Hugh, which he didn't. No need to stand on ceremony with Hugh, thank God. And it would be a real pleasure to see him again after so long. He rated him as one of the best chaps he'd ever met. A man of absolute integrity – and there weren't so many of those around these days. Shame he'd never remarried, but then Laura had been a hard act to follow. He knew that he himself had been very lucky to meet Heather. At fifteen years younger than himself, she kept him younger too, and though it hadn't been quite like the first time around with Anne, he was very fond of her and very content, and grateful, too, for her putting up with an old codger like himself. For preference, he would have stayed in London but when Heather's parents had died and left her the family home she had been very keen to move back there. He knew that the place meant a lot to her. She had been born and brought up in the house and Fossetts had lived there for donkeys' years. It was much too big for the two of them, of course, with their respective children grown-up and gone, and it had needed some sprucing up, to say the least. Holding up, described it better. The trouble was that it cost a small fortune – far more than his pension allowed – which was why they had started the B & B. Heather did the cooking, Mrs Catchpole from the village helped her with the cleaning and his job was to serve the breakfasts and keep the garden under control, including the lake. It was a far cry from his desk-bound banking career, but it was important, he thought, to keep busy in retirement, to keep the cobwebs at bay.

He helped Heather finish in the kitchen and afterwards they made up the beds and put out towels for the coming guests.

'We'll put your Colonel in the Blue Room,' Heather said. 'He should like that.'

The Blue Room – so called because of the faded blue wallpaper – was the nicest, in his opinion. It also had the advantage of being a safe distance from Miss Warner's room so Hugh would be unlikely to encounter her in the corridor, spouting her olde English. The six other guests – all ex-RAF men attending the Buckby Reunion over the weekend – would be sharing the three twin-bedded rooms and the seventh – a last-minute booking – would have to go into one of the former servants' rooms in the attic which had been done up recently.

They quite often had guests who had been stationed at RAF Buckby during the war. Men who came back to take one last look at their past, though the past was vanishing fast. There wasn't much left of the station buildings which were in ruins and smothered by brambles, but the control tower was still standing and so was one of the hangars, and the main runway still existed, along with half the perimeter track.

It was rather a novelty, Geoffrey felt, to have an old wartime airfield at the bottom of the garden. All the land had been owned and farmed by the Fossetts until it had been requisitioned at the start of the Second World War and taken over by the RAF, together with the house. After the war, both house and land had been returned to the family but hard times in the seventies had necessitated selling the land off to a big consortium which had contracted out the farming.

Two of the three runways and half the width of the perimeter track had been taken up to make more room for crops and because concrete fetched big prices as motorway hardcore. The surviving hangar was spared to use for storing corn, the other buildings left to crumble away. Fortunately, the consortium had had no objection to the control tower being preserved by local enthusiasts.

The ex-RAF men who came back to visit often got quite emotional about the old airfield. He'd even seen them weep. It must have been a traumatic time. Flying into hellfire with a snowball's chance of survival, and so many of their comrades dying so young. No wonder they got upset, remembering. They'd had a former rear gunner staying who'd told them he'd had a life expectancy of around forty hours, or five sorties. Even so, the chap had thought he was better off than the bomb aimer who lay prostate in the nose blister and saw the full horror of the flak and flames and other Lancs being blown to pieces.

This Buckby Reunion would probably be the last, he reckoned. The men who had served there weren't getting any younger; in fact, most of them were probably already dead. Anyone who had served in Bomber Command during the war had to be in their late seventies or eighties. Old men, quite a good bit older than himself. Hugh would enjoy meeting them, which was one reason why he'd asked him for this particular weekend. Once those old boys had gone there'd be nobody left to talk about it, first-hand. Nobody who really knew what it had been like. He thought the local committee had done a good job of organizing things. They'd laid on a coach tour of the airfield, followed by lunch in The Grange barn, a dinner at a hotel in Lincoln and a service at the village church on the Sunday to unveil the new memorial window, with a surprise fly-past afterwards. All good stuff. An old soldier like Hugh would be bound to appreciate it as much as the even older airmen.

*   *   *

The Colonel had timed his arrival for late afternoon. He had avoided the motorways and taken a pleasanter, if longer, route on A roads which had led him through the late summer countryside up to Lincolnshire and its vast grid of flat and fertile fields and deep dykes. Bomber County, as Naomi had correctly called it. And he could see why it had been ideal for that purpose. Perched on the very eastern edge of England, it had offered a springboard to enemy-occupied France and Holland across the North Sea. And to Germany.

Guilt at having deposited Thursday in Cat Heaven stayed with him. The old cat had been shocked and outraged as Mrs Moffat had borne him away.

'Don't you worry,' she had said. 'He'll be quite all right. I'll get him settled in and give him a nice supper later.'

It had been impossible to imagine Thursday meekly settling in and he would almost certainly refuse to touch the nice supper. But a day or two could surely do no harm; cats went into catteries all the time and survived. Even so, the guilt kept creeping back. Though there was no real comparison, he was reminded of how he and Laura had felt when they had taken Marcus and Alison to their boarding schools for their first term. The sense of betrayal and abandonment, the terrible wrench of separation. The worry that they would be emotionally scarred for life. As it had happened, both children had thrived, which seemed most unlikely in Thursday's case.

Buckby turned out to be nothing like Frog End. Instead of a cosy collection of houses huddled round a central green, they were spaced out along a straight road, with a brook running fast at the edge.

He found The Grange easily enough, helped by the Bed and Breakfast sign at the gates. Late Georgian or early Victorian, he judged. One of those nice old places that rambled pleasingly and sat perfectly in its surroundings. As he was parking the Riley in the driveway, Geoffrey Cheetham came out of the front door, followed by a black Labrador.

He looked as hale and hearty as he had sounded on the
phone. Older, yes, but weren't they all? They shook hands,
clapped each other on the back.

'Same old car, Hugh?'

'No reason to change her.'

'Quite right. They don't make them like that any more.
This is Monty.'

The Colonel patted the Labrador who had come forward,
tail wagging.

He was conducted, with suitcase, into the house which
was as pleasing inside as it had been outside. It had the
unmistakable look of a proper family home with paintings,
furniture, curtains and carpets that had been unchanged for
many years. The sort of home seldom seen in the modern
world where the main aim was usually to make over and
remodel. As he stood in the hall admiring everything,
Geoffrey's wife appeared and he understood instantly why
his old friend was in such fine fettle. Her good looks owed
nothing to artifice, and the warmth of her smile and of her
welcome were as genuine as her home.

They had tea on the terrace. Proper tea made in a proper
teapot with loose leaves, not bags, and poured out into
proper cups and saucers. There were also cucumber sand-
wiches and home-made sponge cake.

Afterwards Heather Cheetham left them to talk. They
talked, inevitably, of Anne and Laura and of the old days
in post-war Colonial Singapore. The Tanglin Club, Raffles
Hotel, the Cricket Club, curry tiffins, cocktail parties, dinners
and dances. Days which, the Colonel thought, seemed so
very long ago. They had been young then and still years
way from retirement. Life, he remembered, had been very
good. Busy, satisfying, happy. For his friend, he thought,
from the look of him, it probably still was.

'We've got six ex-RAF chaps staying with us for the
weekend for this big Buckby Reunion,' Geoffrey said. 'We
haven't met them before but, apparently, they were all in

the same crew at Buckby. I thought you'd find that interesting, Hugh.'

'Very.'

'I'll take you over to the old airfield later on. It's only a
stone's throw away. The land used to belong to Heather's
family but in the end it had to be sold off and the station
buildings left to fall down. Fortunately, the control tower's
been saved and the main runway is still there.'

'It was a bomber station, I take it?'

'Oh yes. The heavies. Lancasters. Magnificent old beasts,
weren't they? The Battle of Britain Memorial Flight comes
over occasionally in the summer on its way to air shows
and I get a real kick out of seeing their Lanc going past.
As a matter of fact, we've laid on a fly-past for the Reunion
chaps on Sunday – not a Lancaster, of course, but we've
scraped up a Dakota which certainly played its part in the
show. This one was at D-Day and in France and, later on,
it flew in the Berlin Airlift. There's a coach tour of the
old airfield tomorrow morning, and we're doing lunch in
the barn here for them. Heather couldn't cope with that
number on her own, so we've got caterers in to do the
whole thing. And we're going to the Reunion dinner in
Lincoln tomorrow night – you're included as an honorary
guest.'

'That's very kind.'

'Then there's the dedication of a new memorial window
in our church on Sunday.'

'I'll look forward to it.'

'The ex-RAF who served here in the war raised the money
and the village chipped in as well. We think it looks pretty
good. And, apart from the window, we've had a remembrance book done with the names of all the men who died
on ops from Buckby written in it – nine hundred and eighty-
three of them, to be precise. It'll be put on a table under
the window and a page turned each day.'

'That's a lot of men.'

'Well, they only had a one in three chance of surviving a thirty op tour, you know. Poor odds.'

Later on, they walked over to the lake, followed by the dog, Monty, and threw stale bread to the fish. The calm surface erupted into a swirling feeding frenzy and the Colonel wondered uneasily if his charming little pet shop goldfish would eventually grow as big and voracious. He hoped not.

Geoffrey said, 'Your place is called Pond Cottage, Hugh, so you must have a pond.'

'It's a very small one. Nothing like this.'

'Do you have problems keeping the water clear?'

'It was full of weeds and slime to begin with but it's fairly clear now.'

'We've got this confounded blanket weed, as you can see. I've tried everything I can think of to get rid of it but nothing seems to work. I suppose we'll have to get someone in to deal with it at vast expense. That's the trouble with this old place, there's always something that needs to be done.'

'It's a very lovely old place, though.'

'Yes, it is, isn't it? To be honest, I wasn't sure how I'd settle down at first, stuck out in the sticks. But now I find I don't really miss London at all. How about you?'

'The same. I've got rather used to the sticks.'

'And there's something to be said for living in a village, isn't there? The only downside is that everybody else seems to know what you're up to. Do you find that, Hugh?'

He smiled. 'Very much so.'

'Come and look at our bee orchids. They're quite rare, I think.'

The mauve flowers with their furry bee-like bodies were growing in the grass on the bank. The Colonel duly admired them. Orchids in general, with their glacial grandeur, were not his favourite plant but this small, shy, wild example was disarming. He bent down to examine it closer.

*   *   *

Heather Cheetham could see the two men from the kitchen window, inspecting the bee orchids. She had watched them walking round the lake with Monty at their heels, deep in conversation. Geoffrey would undoubtedly have told the Colonel all about the insoluble problem of the blanket weed. In fact, the water had never been clear in all the years she could remember. The lake was spring-fed with a thick mud bottom that got stirred up in certain conditions and there was really nothing much that one could do about it, or the weed. And the house had plenty of its own problems. Leaking roof, gutters rusting, windows rotting, mysterious damp patches appearing on the walls . . . All one could do was to keep applying band aids that cost frightening amounts of money. Of course, there *was* one solution and that was to sell The Grange and so hand over the problems to somebody else with deep pockets. Everything would be solved at a stroke; but it would break her heart.

The truth was that her stubbornness in clinging to her beloved old home was also monumental selfishness and she knew it. The B & B, which had seemed such a good idea at the time, made very little profit which was soon eaten up by the never-ending expense of maintaining the house. It wasn't fair that Geoffrey's hard-earned pension should be used to plug the gaps. And it hadn't been fair, either, to expect him to act as waiter to the guests, or general dogsbody. Not that Geoffrey, bless him, seemed to mind too much – especially if the guests were interesting in some way – but his plans for retirement had been quite different. When she had first met him by chance at a rather stuffy dinner in London, he had been living an uncomplicated life in a pleasant and trouble-free service flat in Fulham; nothing to worry about except how to occupy his days as he chose. For her sake, he had given up that life in exchange for The Grange and all its problems.

She went on watching the two men for a moment – the tall, upright Colonel with his military background, her husband a good bit shorter and a little stooped from years of civilian desk work. They disappeared round the bend in the lake and past the willow tree, heading for the boundary of the old airfield.

If anything could make up for Geoffrey's sacrifice it was having the old bomber station on the doorstep. It thrilled him to bits. And there was a group of like-minded men living in the village who did what they could to keep the control tower in reasonable repair. The idea was that it should be preserved as some kind of memorial – like the new window in the church.

Personally, she found the old airfield a sad place: the bramble-smothered ruins, the potholed perimeter track, the control tower still keeping its lonely and pointless vigil over a runway that no plane would ever use again. Too many ghosts. Too much suffering and sacrifice of young men's lives.

On the way to the old airfield they passed a chicken run where a motley collection of hens was scratching about. They were missing most of their feathers and some had twisted beaks and overlong claws.

'We rescued them from a battery farm,' Geoffrey said. 'There's a Welfare Trust for Hens and they organize it all. I went to collect them last week at a service station on the M11. A woman handed over twenty of the wretched things in a crate. They've spent their lives in wire cages with no room to turn round and nothing to do but lay eggs. These ones are past their best but they'll still lay, given the chance. I'll let them out in the field in a few days' time, once they've got used to things. You won't recognize them in a few weeks. New feathers, new life, new hope, you see. It's the second lot we've rescued. We gave the last ones to Heather's daughter who lives down in Sussex and they're having a fine old time. You ought to try getting some yourself, Hugh.'

'Unfortunately, I have a cat.'

'Oh, they'd probably get along fine.'

Somehow he doubted it. Thursday had never shown the slightest inclination to share his adopted home with any other animal, furred or feathered, or scaled either, come to that. The pet shop goldfish had survived – so far – only because they lived in the pond under water.

He followed his friend through a five-barred gateway and out on to a concrete pathway at the edge of a huge cornfield.

'This is the old perimeter track,' Geoffrey told him. 'It goes all the way round the old airfield but it used to be twice the width. There are the remains of the hardstands where the bombers were dispersed. Wouldn't do to have them all in one place like sitting ducks for the Jerries. He pointed. 'The main runway goes right across the middle of this field where there's that break in the corn, see.' He pointed further into the distance. 'The station offices, ops block, crew briefing room were where those trees are.' More pointing. 'Stores, link trainer, workshops, parachute store, squadron and flight offices, fire tender house, MT shed, photographic block, radar building, gas clothing and respirator store, crew rest and locker rooms. And that old T-2 hangar is used now as a corn store.'

'You seem to know a great deal about the place, Geoffrey.'

'I've got an old map of the site. I've studied it for hours. Fascinating. Of course, there's not much left of the original buildings, but we've done what we can with the control tower. It's still standing and in pretty good nick. If you like, we could walk over and take a closer look.'

They approached the building – a square block of concrete with wide windows at the front of the upper floor and a railed balcony with an outside stairway giving access to the flat roof.

'Care to take a peek inside, Hugh?'

'Certainly.'

Geoffrey produced a key to open the door at the rear.

'Unfortunately, we have to keep it locked against vandals. Yobs come down the runway on their motorbikes after dark and smash windows if they feel like it. God knows what they'd do if they got inside.'

The control tower was an empty shell, all wartime equipment long since removed. On the ground floor, a dark warren of rooms branched off a central passageway. One had been the met office where the teleprinter had been housed, another had been the watch office, another the duty pilot's rest room, another the pyrotechnic stores.

The staircase still bore the words 'Flying Control' on the wall, with an arrow pointing upwards. The Colonel noted, with approval, that there had been no attempt to repaint the sign; the faded black letters and arrow had been left strictly alone. He had seen heavy-handed and regrettable attempts to recolour and restore historic relics which, far from bringing them back to life, had resulted in them being lost for ever.

The signals office and the controller's rest room were at the top of the stairs and beyond them lay the control room, spanning the whole width of the building and flooded with daylight from big windows. An old blackboard was still fixed to one wall, marked with lines for chalking up details of bombing sorties. There was a small table and chair with a visitors' book and a pen.

'The veterans usually sign it when they come back,' Geoffrey said. 'It's quite interesting.' He opened the book at random, turning pages. 'They come from all over, of course. Every corner of the British Isles as well as the Dominions. Poles, too, poor devils, and Czechs.'

Over his shoulder, the Colonel read some of the entries. There was a space for comments but not many had given them – perhaps because the feeling was hard to put into words? The few were to the point. *Sad to see the old place again. Brings it all back. Was it worth it? All those boys dead? We were the lucky ones, God knows why!* Someone had scrawled bitterly: *No thanks! No gratitude! I don't know why we bothered.*

The two men stood in silence for a moment, looking out at the peaceful peacetime view of cornfields.

Geoffrey Cheetham said, 'I come up here quite often on my own – getting away from everything. Spending some time alone and thinking about things – not just the war, but everything, if you understand me.'

'Perfectly.'

The control tower was obviously his friend's equivalent of a garden shed.

'I tell you, Hugh, it gives me goose-bumps sometimes – specially in winter. I even fancy I can hear the bombers. Only the wind, of course. It can get pretty noisy up here when it's blowing hard.' Geoffrey went on staring out of the window. 'Damned brave those chaps. And all volunteers. I wouldn't have wanted to do what they had to do.'

'Nor would I.'

The Colonel had once been inside a Lancaster safely parked on the ground and had pictured for himself how hard it would have been to bail out if the aircraft was hit on a raid. To crawl through the fuselage and clamber over the Beecher's Brook of the main spar in cumbersome flying clothes to reach an escape hatch, while the bomber plunged dizzily earthwards in flames.

'More than fifty-five thousand were lost and thousands more wounded or taken prisoner. Average age of a crew twenty-two, some of them as young as eighteen. Just kids, really. God knows how they carried on but I suppose when you're that young you don't worry so much about dying – you don't think it could ever happen to you.'

The Colonel said drily, 'That's why fighting a war is a young man's game.'

The same went for the army and the navy, he knew, not just the young men in the skies. Despite stark evidence to the contrary, most young men who went over the top, stormed the beaches, braved the perilous oceans, rushed headlong into battles against the enemy on all fronts, did so firmly believing in their own personal survival.

'There were nearly fifty bomber airfields in Lincolnshire by the end of the war, you know Hugh. You couldn't go seven miles without bumping into the RAF.'

'No wonder it's known as bomber county.'

A door led from the side of the control room to the balcony outside and, from there, they climbed the stairway to the flat roof and stood beneath the vast dome of the Lincolnshire skies. Men would have scanned them for the returning bombers. Counted them as they came home from a raid. Noted the ones missing. He wasn't surprised that Geoffrey had imagined hearing engines.

Afterwards they walked across to the old runway. The Colonel looked down the hundred-foot-wide concrete path that had led to the stars. It stretched far into the distance, potholes and cracks infiltrated by grass and weeds and thistles. The Lancaster bombers had taken off from there. Risen up with a great roar of engines, climbing laboriously, burdened by their weight. They would have returned lighter and quieter, hours later. If they were lucky.

They walked back to the house, Monty padding behind.

Geoffrey said, 'Of course, after the war, nobody wanted to know about the Bomber Command chaps. Churchill dumped them, so did the Government and all the Lefties. People said we shouldn't have dropped bombs on the enemy; it wasn't a nice, kind thing to do. So there was no campaign medal, no proper recognition, no thanks. Bloody disgraceful, in my opinion. It was conveniently forgotten about the Germans bombing *us*. About Coventry and London and Portsmouth and Southampton, and about Warsaw and Rotterdam and all the rest, not to mention the small matter of the Nazi death camps and the millions who suffered and died in them.'

'There's talk of a Bomber Command memorial in London.'

'Too little and too late.'

They neared the house.

'By the way, I ought to warn you about Miss Warner, Hugh.'

'Miss Warner?'

'She's another guest we have staying.'

'What do I need warning about?'

'She's rather . . . eccentric. They do a Tudor re-enactment at Buckby Hall every summer and she's taking part. They dress up in period costumes and speak a sort of fake olde English. Miss Warner takes it all very seriously – even at breakfast. It's rather wearing. I thought I'd better put you in the picture.'

The Colonel smiled. 'I appreciate it, Geoffrey. Thanks.'

'I'd be grateful if you'd have your breakfast in the dining room with her.'

'To draw some of the flak, you mean?'

'If you can stand it.'

There were two more cars parked in the driveway alongside his Riley.

Geoffrey said, 'Looks like our crew have already arrived. We'd better go and say hello to them, if you don't mind.'

'It would be a pleasure.'

FOUR

They were standing in the hall, talking to Heather Cheetham. Six grey-haired elderly gentlemen – quietly dressed and quietly spoken.

The Colonel hung back while Geoffrey went to greet them and listened as they gave their names in turn: Jack Davies, Bob Tanner, Roger Wilks, Ben Dickson, Jim Harper, Bill Steed. Good solid English names. It reminded him of the old song about the grey mare carrying all those men to Widecombe Fair: Bill Brewer, Jan Stewer, Peter Gurney, Peter Davy, Dan'l Widdon, Harry Hawk, old Uncle Tom Cobley and all . . . Except that these men hadn't ridden one behind the other on the back of some old nag to go to a country fair in Devon. They had flown on perilous wartime operations in a four-engined heavy bomber over occupied Europe. Remarkable.

He was introduced and shook their hands. It was a privilege to do so. He hadn't met many real heroes.

'I understand you were a Lancaster crew.'

'That's right,' Jim Harper said. 'We did thirty ops together. We don't see each other so often these days, now that we're getting a bit long in the tooth, but we've kept in touch for more than fifty years.'

He was a good bit taller than the others and could have passed for being in his late sixties which he must, in fact, have left some time ago.

'Were you the pilot?'

'No, that's Bill here. I was the navigator. Bob was our flight engineer, Roger our wireless op, Jack our bomb aimer, Ben our tail-end Charlie.'

The rear gunner was the smallest, which made sense; it must have been cramped inside the rear cockpit.

Otherwise, there was nothing about them to give any clues to what they were – or rather – had once been. None of them would have stood out in a crowd, though, in reality, all of them were remarkable men.

Uncle Tom Cobley seemed to be missing.

'I thought a Lancaster had seven in a crew.'

'We're one short, more's the pity. Our mid-upper gunner, Don Wilson, was an Aussie and he went back home after the war. We haven't seen or heard from him for a long time. He may not be alive for all we know.'

Heather Cheetham said, 'That's rather a coincidence. We have a Mr Wilson coming this weekend. A last-minute booking. And he sounded Australian when he phoned.'

The six men looked at each other. The navigator, Jim, shook his head.

'It can't be Don, Mrs Cheetham. He's never made it to a reunion yet. He'd have let us know if he was going to turn up.'

'Well, whoever he is, he's due to arrive later this evening. Would you all like a cup of tea?'

They thanked her politely.

'We haven't been back to Buckby for a few years, Mr Cheetham,' Bill Steed, the pilot, said. 'What's it like now?'

'I'm afraid there's not a lot left. Most of the buildings are in ruins. But we've managed to keep the control tower from falling down and the main runway's still there. We've arranged a coach tour of the air field for you tomorrow morning, so you'll be able to see for yourselves.'

'Yes, we noticed it on the programme. It looks like everyone's gone to a lot of trouble.'

'We want to make you feel welcome, after everything you did for us.'

'Well, we certainly appreciate it. We don't usually get VIP treatment. People are disappointed when they find out we didn't fly Spitfires.'

At that moment the front door opened and they all turned to look at the woman who had come into the hall. She was middle-aged, overweight and dressed in some kind of period peasant costume – long brown skirts, a tightly laced maroon bodice, a white mob cap covering her head. She spread her skirts wide and curtsied low, revealing a mesmerizing amount of cleavage.

'My greetings to you, good sirs. Pray pardon me for this disturbance to your discourse.'

There was a moment's stunned silence before Geoffrey Cheetham collected himself.

'You're not disturbing us at all, Miss Warner. Did you have a good day at the Hall?'

''Twas naught but joy.'

'I'm glad to hear that.' He indicated the former crew. 'These gentlemen are staying with us for the weekend.'

Introductions were made and smaller curtsies bobbed by Miss Warner.

'I am a little weary, I confess, and would fain rest awhile. With your leave, kind sirs, I'll be away to my chamber.'

She curtsied yet again and proceeded towards the stairs. They watched in silence as she scooped up her long skirts over one arm and make her way slowly upwards.

Geoffrey cleared his throat. 'Miss Warner is taking part in the Tudor re-enactment up at Buckby Hall. They hold one every August for three weeks. The idea is to dress and act like someone from those days. She really lives the part, you might say.'

Roger Wilks, the crew's wireless operator, said, 'You mean, she speaks like that all the time?'

'I'm afraid so.'

'My Tudor's a bit rusty.'

'Don't worry. We just talk to her normally. It seems to work all right.'

Geoffrey showed them up to their rooms and the Colonel wandered out into the gardens again. The ex-bomber crew had impressed him deeply. Ordinary men who had done something very extraordinary. Risked their young lives time and time again. They had volunteered to go through hideous danger in order to serve their country and they had apparently done so without complaint or fuss. Service and sacrifice of the highest order. Geoffrey was absolutely right. They had deserved due thanks from the nation after the war, not opprobrium and pointed neglect, which must have been a very bitter pill to swallow. He remembered an RAF bomber squadron insignia that he had once seen, depicting a steel chain with seven links forged into a circle; each link dependent on the others for the strength of the whole. Seven links. Seven men. If all seven held fast, unbreakable.

It would be interesting to see if the remaining mystery guest would provide the missing link.

Later, the crew went off to the local pub, the Fox and Grapes, which they had apparently known well during their time at Buckby.

Heather Cheetham went to the kitchen to cook dinner and the Colonel and Geoffrey had drinks out on the terrace. The August sun was casting a theatrical golden light across the lawn and it was pleasantly warm and very still. England at her best, the Colonel thought. A moment when you completely overlooked the rain and the gloom, the damp and the cold. It was easy to forgive and forget when she could also provide such glorious days.

He had been rather thankful to learn that Miss Warner always took her supper on a tray up in her room.

'Thank God,' Geoffrey had added. 'I can just about put up with her for breakfast, but there are limits. In my view, these re-enactment people are slightly loopy. They seem to take it all so seriously. Heather made me go to the Hall for a day and I couldn't believe it. Do you know, they have more than three hundred volunteers taking part? *Three hundred!* They make their own costumes, even the shoes, and pretend to be Tudor gentry or servants or gardeners, or mummers . . . all sorts of things. Miss Warner is a cook, you know. She bakes bread in the bakery and does it from scratch with live yeast and stone ground flour, and all the rest of it. They mix the dough, then knead it, then leave it to rise, then knock it down and knead it again, then shape it into loaves and leave them to rise again before they're finally shovelled into one of those old baking ovens by the fire. She's told me all about it – at some length, I may say. Be careful not to get her on the subject. They have a dairy as well where other women churn butter and a brewery where men brew ale.'

'Really?'

'*Really*, Hugh. I'm not joking. Last year we had an archer staying here, complete with long bow and arrows which he had up in his bedroom. I rather wondered if it ought to be kept under lock and key like the police insist on with guns. After all it's a lethal weapon, isn't it?'

'Fortunately for England.'

'Point taken. Mercifully, he didn't bother with the Tudor speech – not when he was talking to us, at least. In fact, he didn't say anything much at all except that he wished he'd fought at Agincourt.'

'I can understand that. Stirring times.'

'Very true. Once more unto the breach, and all the rest of it! Well, our bomber crew friends certainly went unto it plenty of times. God, I admire their guts.'

The Colonel said, 'I wonder if your last-minute guest could be their mid-upper gunner?'

'They don't seem to think so. And Wilson's a common enough name.'

'Still, it would be nice to complete the number.'

'All seven together again after so many years? Yes, that would be quite something. Hard to imagine them as they must have been, don't you find, Hugh? Young daredevils, doing that hellish job? They're just quiet old men now.'

'Yes, it's rather hard to imagine.'

'Well, it was a long time ago.'

They ate in the kitchen which suited the Colonel perfectly. The days of sitting at formal dining tables set with fine china, silver and crystal seemed to have vanished from his life and he didn't miss them a bit. It was a pleasure to be in the comfortable old kitchen and eat and chat without any constraints. Laura would have felt the same, he knew. After an excellent pork casserole and apple tart, they had coffee and Geoffrey brought out some brandy and glasses.

'Good health, Hugh.'

The Colonel raised his glass in response to his host and, as they drank, the front door bell jangled loudly.

'It must be our last-minute guest,' Heather said. 'Will you go, Geoffrey?'

They waited and, after a while, Geoffrey came back with the new arrival.

'This is Mr Wilson.'

He was another elderly man, quite short, with sparse grey hair and the lined and leathery face of someone who has spent many years under a hot sun. His suit was crumpled and he wore a brightly patterned tie and when he spoke the Australian accent was unmistakable.

'Sorry to be so late, Mrs Cheetham. Like I was telling your husband here, I took some wrong turns and got lost. Thought I'd never get here. My word, everything's changed since I was last over.'

Geoffrey said, 'Mr Wilson's our crew's long lost mid-upper gunner. We've just been talking about it.'

'I'd no idea they'd be staying here too, Mrs Cheetham. No idea at all.'

Heather said, 'Well, they'll be very pleased indeed to see you, Mr Wilson. And very surprised. They aren't expecting you.'

'I wasn't expecting myself. I had a windfall on the horses

and decided to blow it all on a last trip over here while I could still make it from Australia.'

'The Colonel here is an old friend of my husband.'

'Glad to meet you, Colonel.'

His handshake was firm; his look direct.

Geoffrey said, 'Can I offer you a brandy, Mr Wilson?'

'I never say no to a drink. And the name's Don.'

He sat down at the table, looking round. 'Nice place you've got here, Mrs Cheetham. I'd forgotten how English houses can be. In a class of their own, I reckon.'

'Where do you come from, Don?'

'Sydney. Have you ever been there, Mrs Cheetham.'

'No, I'm afraid we haven't. Geoffrey has spent a lot of time abroad but neither of us has ever been to Australia.'

'How about you, Colonel?'

'Unfortunately not.'

Don Wilson said, 'When I first went back home in '46, it seemed like going to the ends of the earth. Upside down at the bottom of the world – us and the Kiwis on our own together. We'd got the harbour bridge and Bondi beach in Sydney but that was about it. The rest was stuck in a ruddy time warp. Now, you'd never know the place. Skyscrapers, posh hotels, gourmet restaurants, great shopping, not to mention our opera house – though I can't say I've ever been inside. It's as good as any city in the world and a lot better than most. The weather's better too.' He smiled and picked up his glass of brandy. 'But I reckon you've still got something we haven't got – though I'm not too sure I can remember exactly what it is. Perhaps it'll come back to me.'

The Colonel said, 'How long is it since you've been in England?'

'I haven't been here since '46. Couldn't afford to. I couldn't settle down after the war, you see. I bummed around for years. Spent time up in Queensland cutting sugar cane and working in a pineapple canning factory, got married, got divorced, went back to Sydney, tried a few more jobs, got married and divorced again . . . not what you'd call a successful life, Colonel.'

'You had a very successful war.'

He smiled again. 'Yeah, so they say.' He swallowed some brandy. 'Where're my old mates, then?'

'They went down to the local pub for supper,' Heather told him.

'The Fox and Grapes? I remember it all right. Not bad beer and the landlord cashed our cheques even though they bounced like kangaroos. We used to drink there all the time. Our nav and the skipper were officers, and the rest of us were sergeants but we stuck together off the station, as well as on it. All the RAF crews did. It was the way things were in Bomber Command. Not like the Yanks. They never mixed up the ranks, or the colours either.'

'The Fox and Grapes has been done up, I'm afraid. I'm not sure you'd recognize it now.

'Pity. We had some crazy times there. Writing our names on the ceiling, playing the boot game.'

'The boot game?'

'There was a glass boot behind the bar. They'd fill it up with beer and see who'd drink it the fastest. The record was fifty-nine seconds, if I remember rightly. And there was an old piano in the corner with half the notes missing. We stood round it yelling bawdy songs.'

Geoffrey said, 'The glass boot's gone, unfortunately. And the signatures. And the piano.'

'That's a shame.'

Heather looked at her watch. 'I expect they'll be back soon.'

'Don't you believe it! We used to stay till the landlord threw us out.'

But not long afterwards they heard them coming in. Things change inexorably as one gets older, the Colonel thought. No more long drinking sessions, no more late nights. He hadn't actually started on the Horlicks or cocoa routine himself but it could happen.

Geoffrey went out into the hall and the Colonel could hear him asking the six men if they'd had a good evening, but he didn't mention their long-lost mid-upper gunner.

'Come and join us in a nightcap.'

They came into the kitchen and Geoffrey said, with irony, 'I believe you've already met Mr Wilson.'

From his place at the end of the table, the Colonel could see the expressions registering on their faces: disbelief, doubt, amazement – shock, too, if he was not mistaken.

The pilot, Bill Steed, was the first to speak.

'*Don*? Is that you?'

'That's right, Bill. It's me.'

'You've changed a bit. I wouldn't have recognized you.'

'You've changed a bit too, skip. All you Poms have. Good to see you again.'

'We had no idea you'd be here. Why the hell didn't you let us know?'

'Like I was telling these folks, I didn't know I was going to be. I won some money at the races and hopped straight on a plane.'

'You knew about the reunion, then?'

'Yes, I'd run into a bloke in Sydney who was ex-RAF. He lent me a Bomber Command magazine and I read all about it.'

'But why haven't you kept in touch all these years, you bastard? We wrote to you when you first went back.'

'I've never been one for writing letters, Bill – you know that. And I've moved around a fair bit. No fixed address to speak of. Besides, the war was over. Not much sense looking back, was there? Not for us. That's the way I see it.'

There was a pause. The rest of the crew still seemed stunned into silence.

Roger Wilks, the wireless operator said at last, 'Well, it's very good to see you, Don. We just can't believe it, after all this time.'

They were crowding round him now, slapping him on the back, joking, laughing. The whole crew reunited after more than fifty years. Quite a moment! The Colonel had known plenty of service camaraderie during his time in the army and attended a number of reunions, but he doubted if it compared with the fellow-feeling that must exist between men who had flown a tour together in an operational bomber in wartime.

Geoffrey fetched more glasses, more brandy was poured, toasts drunk. Watching them, the Colonel caught occasional glimpses of the young airmen they had once been.

The young-looking Jim Harper came over to speak to him.

'We never thought we'd see Don again. All of us together again after all this time. It's hard to take in. We look bit different, I dare say, but I don't think we've changed much otherwise.'

'You said you were the navigator?'

'That's me. I'd give Bill the course and he had to hope I'd got it right. It wasn't easy, believe me. In those days navs had to do it all with a compass, a ruler and a pencil, and looking out of the window at the stars. Nothing like today. The lads have it easy now. It's all done for them. I was always getting us lost at first, until I got the hang of things. Come to that, we all made a lot of mistakes in the beginning. Bill couldn't do a decent landing, Roger couldn't work the wireless for toffee, our tail-end Charlie, Ben, couldn't have hit a rat in a barrel, Jack couldn't drop the bombs on the target even if I found it for him. Bob, our flight engineer, was about the only one who knew what he was doing.'

The Colonel took it all with a pinch of salt.

'And Don?'

'He was dead-eyed dick, so long as he wasn't too

hung-over. He'd had a lot of practice shooting kangaroos in the outback.'

'Did I hear you taking my name in vain?' The bomb aimer had appeared.

The Colonel looked at him with interest. This was the man who had been lying prone in the forward compartment while the Lancaster had approached the target. He would have had a grandstand view of the hell of flak and flames below, the hideous spectacle of other bombers blown apart or spiralling downwards, and he was the one who had had to give the pilot clear and calm flying orders before he could release the bombs. *Left, left. Right a bit. Steady . . . steady . . . steady. Bombs gone, skipper!* It was hard to imagine it of this mild-mannered old gentleman.

'That's right, Jack. I was telling the Colonel what a useless lot we were at the start. You kept missing the target, remember?'

The bomb aimer smiled slightly. 'So did you, Jim, come to that. I didn't have a hope. Terrible nav you were on those first ops. I don't know how we even got there and back.'

Nor did the Colonel, given the darkness, the atrocious weather, the rudimentary aids, not to mention the enemy flak and the fighters. The thought of those seven very young men – virtually boys – taking a huge bomber into battle over fiercely hostile enemy territory was sobering.

'None of it can have been easy.'

The bomb aimer had stopped smiling. 'It wasn't,' he said quietly. 'But we soon learned.'

Later, he stood at the open window in the Blue Bedroom and looked up at the night sky and a brilliant full moon. A bomber's moon. So-called because, in theory, it had made things easier for the bomber crews during the Second World War. They could see the ground well. By its bright light they could follow the course of rivers, shining like silver ribbons, pick out lakes and landmarks and targets.

In practice, of course, the full moon could just as easily work against them as in their favour. The enemy on the ground could also see *them* and aim their guns the better, and so could the Luftwaffe night fighter pilots. A bomber silhouetted by the moon would have been easy meat. And more than fifty-five thousand men had died.

FIVE

"Tis a fine morning, is it not, Colonel? We are blessed again by the sun's rays.'

Miss Warner was already seated at the table in the dining room when he came downstairs the next morning.

She was dressed, as before, in the white mob cap, full skirts and tightly laced bodice and was working her way through a full English breakfast. The Tudors, he felt, would have approved. Didn't they always start the day off heartily with roasted meats?

'We are, indeed, Miss Warner.'

'Methinks, 'twill last the day.'

'I certainly hope so.'

There was no sign of the crew members as yet and he was not altogether surprised. The reunion celebration in the kitchen had gone on for some time with Geoffrey opening another bottle of brandy. The Australian, especially, had put away a considerable amount.

The Colonel hesitated over where to sit down. The far end of the table might seem rude but to put himself in the front line, close to Miss Warner, could invite a stream of Tudorese. He took the middle course of action and took a chair halfway down its length.

'Didst sleep well, Colonel?'

'Yes, very well, thank you. And you?'

'I passed a most restful night. 'Tis my custom to rise early of a morning. To seize the day. Our little lives have so short a span. We must not waste a moment, must we?'

'That's very true, Miss Warner.'

'Shall you visit the Hall today, Colonel? I wager you would find it of more than passing interest.'

He said politely, 'I'm sure I should, but my day is spoken for.' Very soon, if he wasn't careful, he would find himself talking mock Tudor back to her. 'I've been invited to attend the RAF Buckby reunion this weekend.'

'Ah, yes. Our host hast spoken of it. The gentlemen I encountered last night were once valiant comrades-in-arms, is that not so?'

'Yes, indeed.'

'We are not strangers to combat at the Hall, Colonel. There are skilled archers amongst our numbers. They can be seen drawing their long bows at targets in the grounds.'

'Really?'

'Last year we fought the Battle of Agincourt.'

'Didn't that rather pre-date Tudor times?'

'We were mindful of that fact. 'Twas a celebration of the glorious victory of our noble King Henry V in the year of Our Lord fourteen hundred and fifteen. Many gentlemen took part, armed with bows and swords and carrying banners aloft. The French aristocrats were on horseback, the gallant English yeomen on foot. 'Twas a wondrous sight to behold.'

'I hope nobody was hurt.'

'Only a scratch or two. The English won, of course.'

There had not been much 'of course' about it at the real Agincourt, the Colonel reflected. Any more than there had been in other wars and battles involving the English over the centuries. It had frequently been the nearest run thing, as Wellington had remarked about Waterloo. The same had applied to the Second World War, come to think of it. Triumph eventually snatched from the jaws of disaster. Modern wars seemed to follow a different pattern. They flared up intermittently, or dragged on for many years, or simply petered out unsatisfactorily unresolved.

Miss Warden attacked a pork sausage. 'The year before we did portray the Battle of Hastings.'

'Not exactly a celebration?'

'Yet most historic. And before Hastings 'twas Flodden Field.'

Apparently, battles at the Hall could be refought at random and in no particular sequence.

'And next year?'

'Bosworth, methinks. 'Tis not yet quite decided.'

There were plenty to choose from, he thought. Bannockburn, Crécy, Barnet, Lewes, Evesham, Tewkesbury, Towton . . . Fighting battles had long been bred into the island race. He was about to suggest one of them – possibly Lewes as a complete change of pace and place – when Geoffrey's entrance saved the conversation from descending into farce.

'Good morning, Hugh. What would you like for breakfast? Heather will do eggs anyway you like them, and there's the full English, if you want – fried eggs, bacon, sausages, black pudding, mushrooms, tomatoes.'

'A boiled egg would suit me very well, thank you.'

'How many minutes?'

'About four?'

'Tea or coffee?'

'Coffee, please.'

'There's fruit and cereals on the sideboard, if you'd help yourself.'

He was left alone with Miss Warner once more but fortunately getting his cornflakes provided a diversion and by the time he'd sat down again, six of the valiant comrades-in-arms had appeared. He watched fascinated to see how Miss Warner communicated with them from another century. She proved more than up to it, continuing blithely in her mock Tudor, and to their deep embarrassment.

'Hugh wants a four-minute boiled egg and coffee,' Geoffrey Cheetham told his wife. 'And I just heard the others coming down.'

'That's good. Go and ask them what they'd like, would

you? I need to get breakfast done and cleared away before the caterers arrive. They'll want to take over the kitchen.'

He said, 'We'll be out of your way for the morning while we do the airfield tour. Think you can manage without me?'

She smiled at him. 'Of course I can.'

He paused at the door. 'They're splendid chaps, aren't they? Salt of the earth.'

'The one from Down Under is a bit too salty for me, but the others are very nice indeed.'

She boiled the water for the Colonel's egg and cut some bread for toast. In the beginning, the prospect of cooking breakfast for the B & B guests had given her sleepless nights but practice had made perfect and now it held no fears. She had everything timed to perfection and the Colonel's boiled egg would be served just right. The Aussie would probably want steak with his, in which case he'd be out of luck. Though after the amount of brandy he'd drunk last night perhaps he wouldn't feel like anything. Serve him right!

Miss Warner had finished her breakfast.

'I must away to my baking, gentlemen. I wish you all a merry day.'

They rose to their feet and Roger Wilks, the wireless operator, who was nearest the door hurried to open it for her. Her sweeping curtsy to him was answered by a courtly bow. It was definitely catching, the Colonel decided.

There was a collective sigh of relief as they resettled themselves. The mid-upper gunner had still not come down from his attic bedroom.

'Don was always a lazy sod,' Steed, the pilot, said. 'We used to have to kick him out of bed for ops, didn't we?'

The tail gunner, Dickson nodded. 'Maybe we should do that again. No point missing things when he's come all this way.'

'Speaking of missing things,' Davies, the bomb aimer

said. 'Do you remember when that 109 nearly got us because old Don was having some shut-eye?'

'Dozy bastard!'

They were joking, of course. Their mid-upper gunner must have pulled his weight or they would never have survived. Falling asleep at the switch would never have been tolerated.

They were at the toast and marmalade stage when the Australian finally came downstairs. He was unshaven and his clothes looked as though he had slept in them. Not surprising if he had, considering the combined effect of brandy and jet lag. But his appetite seemed in good order – good enough to see off the big fry-up set before him and to drink several cups of tea.

He said, 'I hear you're coming with us on the coach tour, Colonel. Doesn't sound like there's going to be much left to see, does it? Doesn't surprise me. Most people seem to want to forget what we did. They'd sooner pretend it didn't happen. They feel squeamish about us dropping all those bombs on the Jerries. The fact is we didn't drop nearly enough.'

The Colonel remembered the post-war photographs he had seen of the devastation in German cities.

'I'd say Bomber Command did a pretty thorough job.'

'I was talking about *us,* Colonel. *This* crew sitting round *this* table. We could have killed a whole lot more Krauts, if we'd wanted to.'

The pilot said, 'You always did talk rubbish, Don.'

'But it's the truth, Bill, isn't it? And we all know it, don't we? The Colonel doesn't, though.'

'Put a sock in it, Don. That's enough.'

The Australian shrugged. He drained his cup of tea. 'If you say so. If that's orders. You're the skipper.'

The coach arrived to take them on the tour of the airfield. It was already almost full of other former Bomber Command crew attending the reunion – old men, a few of them with their wives and one with his young grandson. The Colonel found himself sitting beside Roger Wilks, the crew's wireless operator. He was a widower, like himself, and his wife had been dead for nearly fifteen years. He was still trying to get used to living on his own, he said.

The Colonel could sympathize.

'Have you been to other reunions?'

'I used to go to them. I'm getting too old for it now. This'll be my last one. I was twenty when I started on the Lancasters, you know. I'd left school at fifteen and I'd been working in a factory near my home town in Yorkshire. They made glass bottles and jars. Not what you'd call very exciting. When the war started, I volunteered for the RAF and asked to train as a fighter pilot. Of course, I wasn't the only one who wanted to do that but I wasn't good enough to be any sort of pilot, so, in the end, I settled for being a WOP/AG on bombers.'

'It strikes me that all members of a bomber crew were equally important.'

'I don't know about that. I was jack-of-all-trades, to tell the truth. Apart from operating the wireless, I was in charge of the Very pistol so I had to memorize the right colours of the day and remember to switch on the Identification Friend or Foe going out and coming home – that's if we didn't want to get shot down by our own side.'

'Quite a responsibility.'

'Well, some of our ack-ack lads were trigger-happy, I can tell you. It didn't do to give them an excuse. That wasn't all I had to worry about, though. I was lookout in the astrodome and I was the one who got sent to check for hang-ups in the bomb bay and inspect the flare chute to see the photo-flash had gone all right. And I had to wind the trailing aerial in and out by hand which meant crawling on my stomach to get to it. *And* I was expected to know how the intercom system worked and help Jim, our navigator, with the Gee fixes. I also had to learn how to give first aid, as well as look after the carrier pigeon.'

He had forgotten that the RAF used pigeons for sending messages back. It seemed incredible now, given modern means of instant communication. But pigeons had been used routinely during the Second World War and other wars before; some of them, he thought, had even earned medals and, no doubt, thoroughly deserved them.

'You must have been kept very busy.'

'I was. And I did six weeks at gunnery school as part of my training, so I was a gunner too. WOP/AGs they called us, officially. General dogsbody would have been more like it.'

There was a faint trace of grievance, still lingering after more than fifty years.

The coach took them on to the airfield through the original main entrance about a mile down the road from The Grange. They drove round the perimeter track towards the former administrative site where the remains of buildings could be seen, shrouded in brambles and nettles and weeds. Roger Wilks peered out of the window.

'It's hard to tell what's what any more . . . it all looks so different. I can't recognize anything.'

Further on, the driver stopped the coach and they got out. Men who would once have sprung easily from the backs of RAF trucks, now descended steps slowly and stiffly, grasping the handrail. Several of them had walking sticks. Geoffrey had taken on the job of guide and led the way along a path that had been cleared through briars and nettles towards a dilapidated Nissen hut.

The group stopped outside double doors. The wireless operator said doubtfully, 'I think this used to be the crew's briefing room, but I'm not sure.'

They went inside and stood in silence. It was a large rectangular room in a sad state of decay. Brambles groped through broken windows, holes gaped in the corrugated iron roof and weeds sprouted up from the concrete floor. But there were still traces of its former purpose: a dais at the far end with a large blank wall behind it, electric lighting wires trailing from the ceiling, blackout fittings at the windows, stove pipe outlets.

The Colonel had seen enough photographs and old films to picture the scene. There would have been rows of tables and chairs with a gangway down the centre, a target map on the wall behind the dais. At briefings the room would have been crowded with crews, the air thick with cigarette smoke, the atmosphere a mixture of high tension and gallows humour. *Can I have your egg if you don't come back?* The humour was essential, of course. It dispelled fear. Fear was unthinkable. Unadmissable. Nobody actually died on ops. They went for a burton, bought it, got the chop, had their chips, were written off. Anything but killed.

After a while, the reunion group began to move about the room. Bill Steed came over to the Colonel.

'This certainly brings back a few memories.' He pointed to a spot close to the dais. 'Our crew always sat there. Same table, same chairs every time. Two rows back. The room was kept locked all day with a curtain over the map on that end wall there and the windows blacked out, so nobody could see that night's target. We'd bike over early and sit waiting for the Station CO and his lot to arrive. It was a nerve-racking wait, I can tell you. You never knew if it was going to be an easy ice cream op to Italy or a real bastard. When the CO finally turned up they whipped away the curtain and showed you the red tape pinned across the map. Then you knew what you were in for. Essen, Cologne, Stuttgart, Hamburg – they were always bad ones but Berlin was the worst, we thought. The Big City, we used to call it. Old Yellowstripe. More than a thousand miles there and back and better defended than any of them. Radar, decoy targets, and flak thick enough to get out and walk on. And if it wasn't the flak, we'd have swarms of Jerry night fighters. The bastards would go for our blind spot under the fuselage.'

'Did you get hit?'

'They clipped us a few times, but we got away with it. The Lancaster's an amazing plane, you know. Some of them made it home on two engines and with more holes than a kitchen colander. Others weren't so lucky.'

It was a casual comment but the Colonel had been used to those during his time in the army. Phrases like rather tricky, a spot of bother, a bit of a problem, were used. In his personal experience, no soldier had ever overdramatized a situation, or ever expressed the sheer terror that he may well have felt. No doubt airmen were much the same. He had heard about the rare cases of LMF among the bomber crews – lack of moral fibre as it had been termed. Cowardice, by a less forgiving name. The men in question had been swiftly removed before they demoralized others and been demoted to menial tasks and lifelong disgrace. Fortunately, such traumas were better understood today and dealt with more mercifully.

The ex-skipper went on, with bitter irony. 'At the end of the briefing, the CO used to stand up to give us his pep talk. Maximum effort is expected, gentlemen! I'm counting on all crews to do their utmost! Hit the Hun hard tonight! Knock Berlin flat! All very well for *him*; he didn't have to go there. He was tucked up safe and warm in his bed while we were out busy bombing munition factories, steel-works, industrial areas, railway yards . . . Tearing the black heart out of Germany was how Bomber Harris put it. We thought a lot of Harris, you know. He knew what war was about and we respected him. Killing the enemy or dying yourself.'

That just about summed up the situation, the Colonel thought. Kill or be killed.

He said, 'Well, you did an extraordinary job.'

'We did our best, that's all.'

'As pilot, you would have had the hardest job. The greatest responsibility.'

He shook his head. 'I depended on them, just as much as they depended on me. We understudied for each other. If one of us was put out of action, someone else had to be able to take over, at least well enough to get us home. I trained Bob, our flight engineer to fly the Lanc straight and level and to put her down on the ground in an emergency. We were all in it together.'

'Life must have seemed rather boring afterwards.'

'Oh, no. I was just very glad to be alive. Excuse me, Colonel. I ought to join them.'

He watched the skipper walk over to his former crew to stand at the very spot where they had waited many times to learn their fate: an ice cream op or a bastard. As it happened, they had formed a symbolic circle: the seven links in that unbreakable chain. Grim-faced. Remembering.

Remembering was what such reunions were all about, the Colonel thought. Remembering not only old comrades but also one's youth. Recapturing, for a while, what it had been like to be young and fit, fighting for something worth fighting for. Unlike other conflicts, the Second World War had been a clear case of Good versus Evil. A simple, straightforward choice. For many men the experience must have been the most intense and thrilling part of their lives. Something to be quietly proud of: a satisfaction of duty done in the face of extreme danger. Nobody and nothing could ever take that away from the Bomber Command crews. The fighter pilots may have had the glamour and the glitz and the glory, but the steadfast, unassuming bomber boys had done more than their share for victory. They had nothing to apologize for. Nothing to doubt. Nothing to regret, except for the sad loss of those of their number who had missed out on life.

There was such a thing, he knew, as survivors' guilt.

Some men found it hard to come to terms with living when so many comrades had died. Why had they been the lucky one? What had they done to merit it? There was no easy answer.

After the briefing room, the group toured what was left of other old buildings – the flight office, parachute store, photographic block, workshops . . . all in a similar state of near-ruin.

'I can't recognize anything any more,' Roger Wilks kept saying. 'Everything's changed.' He looked upset.

Perhaps it was a mistake to try to go back, the Colonel thought. As had been so accurately observed, the past was a foreign country where things were done differently. It could be remembered, but it could never be brought back, or relived, or changed.

They climbed back into the coach to drive round to the control tower which, at least, was recognizable and no such disappointment. Up in the control room, the Australian stood by the Colonel at one of the big windows overlooking the runway.

'Weird to see it so quiet now,' he said. 'It wasn't like that in our day. On ops nights we'd be queued up all round the peri track, making a hell of a racket. When it was our turn to take off they'd give us the green light and we'd roar down that runway over there, loaded with bombs and fuel and wondering if we were going to get airborne or finish up in a fireball, like we'd seen happen to some poor blokes. There were always some WAAFs and penguins from admin waving to us from the sidelines and they'd turn out in all weathers. I used to think it was a pretty nice thing to do. Them all waving away at us as we went by and the worse the target, the harder they waved. Sometimes they'd smile, too. Mind you, they'd got something to smile about . . . they weren't going with us. I remember it all like yesterday, clear as anything. You don't forget your war, do you? What you made of it, and what it made of you. I've never forgotten, see, because I've plenty to remember. And none of it too good.'

'Is that why you've never been back until now?'

'You could say that. Bad memories, and no money.'

'But you were very lucky with your crew.'

'Without them, I wouldn't be standing here today. And that's a fact. We were still kids, you know. Ben was eighteen, I was nineteen, Roger and Jack were twenty, Bill and Jim were both twenty-one and Bob was an old, old man of twenty-three.'

Bob, the Colonel remembered, was the only one who had got everything right from the first. A serious-looking man, as befitted his senior years. The flight engineer had to be reliable. He sat next to the one and only pilot and understood the engines. He could fly the Lancaster straight and level and, at a pinch, he could land her.

'You were all very young.'

'We weren't foolish, though. Do you know how RAF crews got together in those days?'

'No, I don't.'

'They put you all in a hangar – pilots, flight engineers, navigators, bomb aimers, air gunners, wireless ops – so you were milling around like a lot of sheep at market. Then this officer gets up on a chair and tells us to 'sort yourselves out, chaps'. And he gets down and leaves us to get on with it. You just went for whichever blokes looked like a good bet and hoped you didn't pick any duds.'

The Colonel smiled. 'That sounds as good a way as any.'

'Yeah . . . Birds of a feather, you could say. And our little lot flocked nicely together.'

Bill Steed wandered over. 'Shooting a line, as usual, Don?'

'No, skip. Matter of fact, I was just telling the Colonel how we crewed up. You and me first, wasn't it? Like picking partners for a waltz. Then we ran into Jack and Jim who'd already got together. And, after that, Roger came up. That was when we were still on Wellingtons, though. Later on, Bob and Ben joined us when we converted to the heavies. So, finally, we had ourselves a Lancaster crew. We got it all worked out just the way we wanted. Isn't that right?'

The skipper nodded. 'Yes, Don. That's right.'

'You and Jim were officers, the rest of us sergeants, but we were all equal, weren't we?'

'Indeed, we were.'

'No saluting, was there? First names from the start. And we all went off to the pubs together. Remember the time that new barmaid wouldn't serve us sergeants in the lounge bar? Officers only, she said. You can't drink in here. So, you and Jim put down your beers and walked out with us.'

'Yes, I remember.'

'The landlord came and apologized when you'd had a word in his ear. Free drinks all round after that.'

They had stood by each other, off duty as well as on. The Australian had talked about it before, the Colonel remembered. They'd gone out together and drunk together and played crazy games together in the pub, like the glass boot game. And they would willingly have died together, if luck had not been on their side.

The rear gunner, Ben Dickson, was standing alone at the next window. The youngest and the smallest. Eighteen was no age to have been doing that grim job. The rear cockpit was generally considered, so the Colonel had heard, to have been the worst place in the Lancaster. Lonely and cramped and cold, and the rear turret would have been an easy target for enemy fighters. The chances of crawling out of the cockpit and back into the fuselage to reach an escape hatch can't have been too good.

He walked over to have a word, but was ready to retreat at once if the man preferred to be left alone with his thoughts. The rear gunner turned, though, and nodded to him. He pointed.

'The main runway's just over there, where you can see the break in the crops.'

'Yes, I've walked down it. A remarkable sight.'

Ben Dickson said drily, 'I know it backwards. Facing the other way, see. I was the first of the crew to be airborne as the tail went up, and when we came back I was the last to land – unless the skipper did a greaser.'

'A greaser?'

'All three wheels touching down at once, including the one under the rear cockpit. It didn't happen too often.'

The Colonel said, 'Not a very comfortable place to be in any case.'

'That's an understatement. The cold was bad enough to start with and then they went and took out the centre Perspex panel so we could see without all the misting and icing-up, and it got even worse. We had heated flying suits but they were always conking out. I can tell you it wasn't much fun. Hours and hours of freezing cold on the long ops and I used to get terrible cramp, too.' The rear gunner shrugged. 'Of course, us crews were just what you in the army used to call cannon fodder. The ones in charge didn't care much about us because if we got killed, there were plenty of others to take our place.'

That might have been true in the First World War trenches, the Colonel agreed, but he didn't believe it had been so in the Second. It had been expected that men would have to die but they had not, so far as he was aware, ever been considered expendable.

He noticed that there had been the same bitterness in the gunner's tone as there had been in Roger Wilks's at being a dogsbody and in their skipper's over the station CO's blustering briefing pep talks. Perhaps they also all resented the shabby way the bomber crews had been treated, post war, in terms of official recognition. Nobody could blame them for that. They must have felt bitter for themselves and for the thousands who had died.

He said, 'It's good to see that you are being properly appreciated now.'

'Yes, they've been changing their tune lately. But it's too late for most of us, isn't it?'

SIX

The coach brought them back round the perimeter track to the gate that led to The Grange. As they climbed out again a bagpiper in full Highland dress, standing at the foot of the steps, began to play. He led the veterans in a slow procession to the barn where the lunch was being held and their route was lined with people from the village clapping them. The Colonel, who had detached himself from the group, joined in the applause. He saw that a number of the veterans had tears in their eyes.

The barn had been decorated with RAF and Union Jack flags and trestle tables had been covered with white cloths, name cards at each place. Somewhat to his embarrassment, the Colonel discovered that he had been put at the top table between a retired Air Vice-Marshal and a parish councillor. The Air Vice-Marshal had served post war at Buckby and had fond memories of the station.

'Cold as hell in the winter, uncomfortable, inconvenient, ankle-deep mud . . . but I was very sad when it was finally closed down. It played a big part in the war, as I expect you already know.'

'I'm afraid I'm a complete stranger to Buckby. I'm here under entirely false pretences.'

'Well, so am I, come to that. I didn't get here till the sixties. We had it easy compared with what these wartime chaps had to go through. It's good to see them getting some proper recognition at last. They deserve every bit of it. Brave men. They did what they were asked to do. Got on with a ghastly job without any fuss. Hats off to them, I say.'

The parish councillor on the Colonel's other side was about the same age as the Air Vice-Marshal but had no

Service memories of his own. He had lived in Buckby for most of his life and remembered it vividly as a child in wartime.

'Our cottage was on the other side of the aerodrome and my brother and I used to watch the bombers whenever we could. And if we saw a whole lot of them going out on to the perimeter track we knew it was going to be a big raid. We'd count them out and we'd count them back. When they took off their engines roared like lions but when they came back, free of the heavy load, they sounded quite different – singing, not roaring. If there was a moon shining we'd leave the bedroom curtains open and when we saw a shadow move across the wall we knew it was another Lancaster coming in to land, safe home again.'

The councillor was a member of Geoffrey Cheetham's group of enthusiasts who had put in many hours of work on the control tower.

'We're glad to do it. Otherwise there'd soon be almost nothing left of RAF Buckby, which would be a great pity. People are interested, you know. Kids today want to know what grandad did in the war. More and more of the old war birds are being restored and flown at air shows in front of big crowds. And it's not just about the fighters, people want to see the bombers too. Thank God, we've still got the control tower here to show them and now we'll have our memorial window and remembrance book in the church as well. It's the least we can do.'

The Colonel looked down the two long tables. He could see Bill Steed's crew sitting together at the end of one of them. The Australian gunner was draining his glass of beer and held it out for a refill. By the look of him, it was far from the first time.

At the end of the lunch, Geoffrey stood up to make a short speech of welcome. He finished with thanks.

'To all you who served at RAF Buckby during the Second World War, we would like to express our gratitude, and to remember those of your comrades who sacrificed their lives in the cause of the freedom that we enjoy today.'

There was prolonged applause. Some of the village boys had sneaked into the barn and were going round the tables, collecting autographs.

Not from footballers, for once, the Colonel thought. Nor from tennis players, or athletes, or cricketers, or actors, or TV celebrities. From old men with unknown names and unknown faces but whose courageous deeds were finally being properly understood and appreciated. The Australian, Don Wilson, was signing his autograph with a grand flourish, the rest of his crew rather more modestly but he could see that they were all gratified by the admiration and the attention.

The lunch over, the veterans were driven off in the coach and the locals dispersed to their homes. Bill Steed and his crew squashed themselves into the dinghy and took it out on The Grange lake. The Colonel and Geoffrey Cheetham watched them from the bank.

'They may have been able to fly a bomber,' Geoffrey said. 'But they haven't a clue how to row a boat.'

The Australian had grabbed the oars and jammed them in the rowlocks. He was sitting facing the bows and when he realized his mistake he stood up to turn round the other way and the dinghy rocked and rolled, shipping water. Eventually, the navigator, Jim Harper, wrested the oars away from him and the gunner was dumped, protesting loudly, in the stern.

Geoffrey frowned, 'I hope they can all swim.'

'Is it deep?'

'About ten or twelve feet in the middle. Deep enough to drown. Still, the boat's a pretty safe old thing. Very hard to capsize.'

They watched the dinghy's progress across the lake. The navigator was getting the hang of rowing and seemed to know where he was going – as, indeed, he should have done. The rest of them had redistributed their weight to balance the boat while the Aussie, fortunately, stayed slumped in the stern.

'We'd better make sure they get back all right, Hugh.'

They sat down on a bench and went on watching while the seven elderly men went round and round the small lake, like children having innocent fun. The Colonel thought it was a rather poignant sight.

At last they came back to the wooden jetty and the mooring post.

More rocking and rolling as they clambered out while Geoffrey and the Colonel held the boat steady. Don Wilson had fallen asleep in the stern and had to be woken and levered with care on to the jetty. The pilot and the bomb aimer supported him between them, one on each side.

Bill Steed said, 'We'll take him upstairs to get some shut-eye before the dinner tonight.'

'Need some help?'

'No thank you, Colonel. We're used to it. Don could never hold his drink.'

They went off across the lawn, their mid-upper gunner dragged along between them. As they neared the house, Miss Warner appeared and stood open-mouthed as they passed her.

Geoffrey groaned, 'Oh God, she's coming our way.'

'We could always take the boat out again.'

'Good idea, Hugh. Hop in quick.'

They pushed off, Geoffrey seizing the oars, and rowed fast towards the centre of the lake. By the time Miss Warner had reached the bank, they were safely out of earshot.

SEVEN

The reunion dinner was to be held that evening in a banqueting room at a hotel in Lincoln. Don Wilson had sobered up enough for his comrades to take him along with them in one of their two cars while the Colonel drove Geoffrey and Heather Cheetham in his Riley.

The three towers of the cathedral stood out clearly on the hilltop as they approached the city. A very useful landmark for any aircraft trying to find its way home at dawn in bad weather, the Colonel thought. And God only knew how they had managed it at night. *Hallo Darky*, he knew, had been the wartime emergency call sign of a bomber in trouble.

Hallo Darky, Hallo Darky. Mayday, Mayday, Mayday. A soft-voiced WAAF would have answered calmly out of the night. *Hello, aircraft calling Darky. Transmit for fix.*

To an exhausted pilot returning with a badly shot up aircraft and probably with wounded or dead on board, it must have seemed like the voice of an angel.

Pre-dinner drinks were being served when they arrived and the gathering included city dignitaries with their wives, a local reporter, a press photographer and ordinary civilians, some of them about the age that the crews would have been during the war.

'We had to limit the numbers or we'd have been swamped.' Geoffrey said. 'There's been a lot of interest from all over the county. Now, more than ever, apparently. Strange, isn't it?'

The Colonel didn't think it was strange at all. The men of Bomber Command might have been cold-shouldered by post-war governments but, by now, ordinary people were well aware of the guts and grit that they had demonstrated.

The steadfast bravery that they had shown unflinchingly for nights on end. They had been a big part of England's finest hour. An hour to be proud of – unlike some others since.

Before the dinner started there was a photocall for the veterans who lined up dutifully, blinking in the flashlights, unused to being treated like film stars. Spontaneous applause broke out, everyone clapping them loudly. Being the only surviving complete crew, Bill, Jack, Bob, Roger, Ben, Jim and Don came in for special attention and a photograph on their own, the Australian having been persuaded to put down his beer. There was more applause.

The seating was at round tables and the Colonel had been placed next to Heather Cheetham. The older woman on his other side was very small and thin but far from frail. Sprightly was the adjective he would have used. Even tough. She had served in the Air Transport Auxiliary in the Second World War, she told him. Her job had been to collect and deliver planes all over the country. There had been more than a hundred women serving. They had flown in daylight within sight of the ground, with no radio, following a map balanced on their knee and a book of pilot's notes for the aircraft type. She had flown many different kinds: Hurricanes, Spitfires, Sea Otters, Walruses, Oxfords, Blenheims, Lysanders, Mustangs, Corsairs . . . and even the four-engined Lancasters.

'Weren't they rather heavy for you to handle?'

She smiled drily. 'I managed. They gave me some phone directories to sit on and I was allowed to take an ATC cadet to twiddle the knobs I couldn't reach. A lad between twelve and fourteen. You should have seen the faces of some of the RAF when we delivered a Lanc and I stepped out, followed by a mere boy. Just the two of us. Their jaws dropped.'

She amused him with more stories of the perils of flying for the ATA. The weather, of course, had been one of the biggest hazards, and also the thick hawsers tethering the barrage balloons which were unmarked on maps. Another danger was from being shot at by their own side which had happened to her a number of times.

'I didn't blame them too much. Aircraft recognition is tricky, especially in poor visibility.'

It was generous of her, he thought, wondering what a returning Lancaster crew might have made of the same experience after a gruelling operation over enemy territory. Roger Wilks, the wireless operator, had not seemed to share her understanding attitude. He had referred to the ack-ack crews as trigger-happy which would probably be one of the milder terms used.

To his left, Heather Cheetham said, 'Our Australian seems to be knocking it back again. I do hope he doesn't cause any trouble.'

Don Wilson was at an all-male table, somehow separated from the rest of his crew and holding court. The men sitting with him were hanging on to his every word and the Colonel guessed that they were local enthusiasts. The kind who would spend all their spare time exploring old wartime airfields, hunting for relics, devouring books and magazines on the subject.

The table was too far away for the Colonel to hear what the Australian was saying but he was certainly saying plenty. Somebody refilled his glass, and, a few moments later, it was being refilled again. And again. Some of the contents had spilled down the front of his shirt.

Towards the end of the dinner, the Air Vice-Marshal who had sat next to the Colonel at the barn lunch rose to his feet to speak about the veterans present and what they had done for their country. It was a powerful speech and the toast, when he had finished, was to absent friends. All those thousands, the Colonel thought.

People began to leave while others, including Don Wilson, gravitated to a bar set up in the same room. The numbers surrounding him had grown and they had now been joined by the local reporter who was taking notes and by the press photographer who was aiming his camera. Someone pressed yet another drink into the Australian's hand. He was swaying on his feet, his drink sloshing to and fro in its glass.

Geoffrey Cheetham said, 'Do you think we should take him home, Hugh? Before he gets any worse.'

'I think his skipper's about to do that.'

Bill Steed had approached the group, and the other five members of the crew were not far behind him. They did the difficult job very well, the Colonel thought. Quietly, tactfully and without any fuss, the Australian was extricated and shepherded out of the room.

The reporter closed his notebook. He caught the Colonel's eye and shrugged.

'Pity about that. I'll have to catch him tomorrow when he's sobered up.'

'It would be better.'

'Amazing guy! Full of great stories.'

'Yes, I'm sure.'

'I'm doing a piece for my paper about the old vets: "Forgotten Heroes."'

'I wouldn't say they were forgotten.'

'No, not by this lot. But ask kids today what RAF Bomber Command did in World War Two and most of them haven't a clue. They've seen the film of the Dam Busters and they know the march, but that's about it.' The reporter put away the notebook. 'The Aussie's going to the memorial service tomorrow, so I'll fill in the blanks then. By the way, what's creepback, do you know?'

'Creepback? No, I'm afraid I don't.'

'Well, he was talking about it . . . something to do with bombing. He wasn't making much sense, to be honest. I'll ask him tomorrow. Use it in the article if I can.'

The Colonel finished his drink and went in search of Geoffrey and Heather. The farewells took some time but eventually they left the hotel and drove back to The Grange.

Another bomber's moon lit their way, riding high in the sky.

'Well, it all went pretty well, don't you think, Hugh?'

'Yes, I do. A wonderful success.'

'Pity about Wilson. Drunk as a skunk again.'

'I don't think it mattered too much. His crew dealt with it very well.'

'Still, it rather let their side down.'

He turned the Riley in through The Grange gateway. The three visiting cars were parked neatly by the front door, together with the runabout used by Miss Warner, who was evidently prepared to compromise over Tudor modes of transport, if nothing else. The hall and landing lights were on, but the rest of the house was in darkness. Everyone had gone to bed and Monty was asleep in his basket beside the Aga. Heather Cheetham went straight upstairs while the Colonel and Geoffrey lingered over a whisky.

'I think you'll approve of the memorial window when it's unveiled tomorrow, Hugh. It's rather fine. Captures the essence of things, if you know what I mean.'

'I'm looking forward to seeing it.'

'The service kicks off at eleven a.m. but we'll need to leave here by ten thirty, if you don't mind. I need to get there in good time. We can walk – it's not far.'

'That's fine by me.'

'I'll be rather sorry when this weekend is over, you know. It's been a hell of a lot of work, but it's been worth it. I feel we've paid our dues.'

'And I think it's been much appreciated.'

'Yes, I get that impression. They're a fine bunch, aren't they – our veteran visitors? Decent. Modest. Unassuming. Except maybe for our Australian friend. He seemed to be shooting his mouth off this evening, didn't he?'

'I'm not sure that he was making much sense to anybody.'

'Well, let's hope he doesn't repeat the performance tomorrow.'

The Colonel considered his glass thoughtfully. 'What's creepback, Geoffrey?'

'Creepback?'

'An RAF bombing expression, apparently. According to the local newspaper reporter, Don Wilson was talking about it.'

'Never heard of it. Why?'

'Oh, I was just wondering.'

'Ask the others in the morning. They ought to know.'

EIGHT

The Colonel was first down to breakfast, beating Miss Warner by a short head. He had hardly sat down when she appeared in the doorway in full Tudor rig.

'Another fine morning, is it not? Are we not fortunate in being so blessed?'

He rose to pull out her chair for her. 'Yes, indeed, Miss Warner. We most certainly are.'

'I trust you all supped well?'

'Yes, thank you.'

She glanced up at him playfully.

'Methinks, some of you rather too well, perhaps, Colonel? I was aroused from my slumbers.'

She must have heard the crew hauling their drunken mid-upper gunner up the stairs to bed.

'I'm sorry if you were disturbed.'

'It does not signify. 'Twas but for a moment.'

'Can I bring you some cereal?'

'What kindness! Perhaps some flakes of corn.'

He fetched the little individual box of Kelloggs and set the milk jug in front of her.

'You will not partake yourself, sir?'

'No. No cereal for me this morning.'

'Then I must perforce eat alone.'

Again, mercifully, Geoffrey appeared to take the cooked orders – the full English for Miss Warner, a boiled egg and toast for himself. One tea, one coffee.

'What does the day hold for you, sir? Good things, I trust.'

'There's a service at the village church this morning. To unveil a memorial window.'

'Ah, yes. I have heard talk of this. The sacrifice of brave
warriors is to be honoured in this way. 'Tis most fitting.
Would that I could attend myself but duty calls me to the
Hall. Bread must be baked. Work done.'

'Couldn't you take some time off?'

'Mercy, no! I am but a humble servant to the gentry. I
am at their bidding.'

The gentry, presumably, just sat around all day giving
orders.

'Perhaps it would be nicer to be one of them next time?'

She looked shocked. 'We have all been given our station
in life, Colonel. 'Tis the will of our Lord and we must needs
be content.'

He said gravely, 'Yes, of course.'

They were halfway through the full English and the boiled
egg before the others came down – or at least six of them.
Apparently, the mid-upper gunner was still out for the count.
The skipper had banged loudly on his door but without
getting an answer and it had been decided to let him sleep
it off. The Colonel thought it was a sound idea. Always let
sleeping drunks lie.

'We had a real struggle getting him up to bed last night,'
Bill Steed said. 'I hope you didn't hear us, Miss Warner?'

'I did, indeed, sir.'

'I'm very sorry. We tried to keep as quiet as we could.'

'Pray do not trouble yourselves. 'Twas of little account.
I was soon sleeping peacefully once more.'

She went off to do her baking and at half past ten the
rest of them assembled in the hall. Church parade,
the Colonel thought. Six old airmen and one old soldier,
spruced up in their best with highly polished shoes. Just
like old times.

The village church was filling up fast when they arrived
and the congregation included several senior RAF officers
in uniform. The veterans were shown to seats in the front
rows, as honoured guests, many of them wearing medals

pinned to their civilian clothes. No campaign medal, though, since none existed. A disgraceful omission, the Colonel thought.

The hymns were well chosen: *Thy Hand, O God, Has Guided, For All the Saints,* and, almost inevitably, *Jerusalem.* The vicar rose to the occasion with an excellent sermon and appropriate prayers.

Let us remember before God, and commend to his sure keeping, all those who served our country in the Second World War. We especially remember today those from RAF Buckby who willingly laid down their lives in the cause of our freedom. And we pray for all whom we knew, all whose memory we treasure and all whose courage we revere.

Towards the end, the new memorial window was unveiled by the widow of an RAF sergeant pilot killed over Germany in 1944. She then opened the first page of the remembrance book.

When the service was over and the congregation were filing out, the Colonel went to take a closer look at the stained glass window which depicted a bareheaded young man in RAF flying clothes and wearing a Mae West and parachute harness. He was standing looking up at the golden and glorious figure of a robed angel whose kindly hands were outstretched down towards him. It was simple and symbolic. After all, there was a strong angelic connection. Angels also had wings to soar aloft. *They shall bear thee up lest at any time thou dash thy foot against a stone.* And not for nothing was altitude in slang RAF flying terms measured in angels. An angel was a thousand feet, angels one five was fifteen thousand. The famous fighter pilot's poem about dancing the skies and putting out his hand to touch the face of God was powerful stuff but the slower, lower bomber crews had had the angels rooting for them too.

The book of remembrance lay open on a table beneath the window, the names written in copperplate handwriting.

John Gilman, Peter Morris, Arthur Knight, Stephen Watson, Michael Harrison, Richard Slater . . . It was one of the saddest things, the Colonel thought, to see hard, cold evidence of lives lost that had barely begun, whether it was names written in a book, or carved in stone, or the sight of row upon row of white graves reaching into the far distance.

He joined the congregation who were streaming out into the sunshine. Right on cue, a Dakota came into view, flew low over the church and circled twice before it went away. Not a Lancaster, but, as Geoffrey had rightly pointed out, the DC-7 had certainly played its part in the show. A tireless workhorse: troop carrier, cargo transporter, glider tower, present at all the major conflicts of the war: Arnhem, North Africa, Sicily, D-Day, the Battle of the Bulge, crossing the Rhine, out in the Far East . . . and later, at the end, bringing the POWs home.

The retired Air Vice-Marshal he'd encountered at the lunch and dinner was standing beside him, watching the Dakota.

'Damned fine aeroplane.'

'One of the best,' the Colonel agreed.

'Eisenhower said it was one of the four most vital machines in the war, you know.'

'What were the other three?'

'In his opinion, the bulldozer, the jeep and the two-and-a-half ton truck.'

'It's hard to argue with that.'

'All plodding workhorses, of course, but we couldn't have coped without them. Modern warfare's a totally different kettle of fish, isn't it? We can programme weapons to land on a sixpence now, whereas in the old days it was hit and miss, and, from what I gather, rather a lot of miss. Those Bomber Command crews did a wonderful job but it can't have been easy to hit anything accurately at night and with so few aids, and under heavy fire.'

The Colonel said, 'I've been wondering what the term

creepback meant in bombing terms. I've never heard it used before.'

'During a long raid, crews sometimes tended to drop their bombs progressively shorter and shorter of the primary target. It was called creepback.'

'Did it happen often?'

'Not as far I know. And it wasn't deliberate, of course. I imagine there was the odd crew who would get rid of their bombs early so that they could turn back but that's quite a different matter. There are always the few who'll find ways to save their own skins, aren't there?'

He'd known men like that in the army, but only a very few. None of the Bomber Command men whom he'd met had struck him as that sort. Quite the contrary.

The reporter who had spoken to him after the dinner, came up.

'I've been looking everywhere for that Aussie. He doesn't seem to have shown up.'

'He was sleeping-in this morning.'

'I'm not surprised. Those diggers can certainly put it away. Do you know where I can get hold of him?'

'He's staying at the same place as myself. I could give him a message, if you like.'

'That'd be good. Here's my card so he can give me a buzz when he's surfaced. I'd like to use him in my article. He'd got lots to say and isn't shy about saying it, unlike some of the other old boys.'

The Colonel put the reporter's card away in his pocket. 'Well, the rest of his crew are standing just over there, if you want a word with them.'

'That's a stroke of luck.'

The reporter hurried over, notebook at the ready, and the Colonel watched him asking eager questions and Bill Steed and his crew giving wary answers.

Since Geoffrey and Heather were busy chatting with people, the Colonel decided to walk on back to the house.

Monty was lying by the front door and got up to greet him. There was no sign of the Australian.

He wandered over towards the lake, Monty following. At the bank some fish turned up, circling hopefully, mouthing at the surface. One of them, in particular, caught his eye – a silver-white fish much larger than the others. A ghost carp, he thought, and well named. It appeared and disappeared gliding silently through the blanket weed. Sinister. He much preferred his own bright little pond fish darting about.

Monty had gone off round the bend in the lake and started to bark and, eventually, the Colonel went to investigate. The dog was barking at something half submerged in the water twenty feet or so away from the bank. A dark mass partly obscured by the weed that, at first, he mistook for some rags – until he made out the protruding arms and the pale flesh of hands. And then he saw the empty dinghy caught up in the reeds by the bank and the oars floating free on the surface.

NINE

The rags were Don Wilson. He was floating face down and, though he was quite a small man, it was a tricky job for the Colonel to haul his waterlogged body out on to the bank. All attempts to revive him were hopeless; he had clearly been dead for some hours.

The Australian was wearing the same suit and garish tie that he had arrived in and worn to the dinner. The tie was loose around his neck and there were beer stains down the front of the white shirt. No shoes, though, and a large hole in the heel of his left sock. A sad end, the Colonel thought, looking down at him. All deaths were sad but there was something very pathetic about this one.

He looked up to see Geoffrey and Heather running towards him, followed by Wilson's crew. They stood staring down at the Australian. Geoffrey put his arm round Heather.

'What in God's name happened, Hugh?'

'I don't know. Monty started barking and when I went to see what the trouble was I saw something floating in the water. When I realized what it was I went in and got him out. I tried to revive him but I'm afraid it's far too late. The dinghy's over there in the reeds. It looks as though he must have taken it out and fallen overboard.'

Bill Steed said, 'He wanted us all to go out on the lake again when we brought him back from the dinner last night. He went on about it being a bomber's moon – just like on some ops in the old days. Of course we didn't take any notice. We took him straight upstairs and put him to bed.'

'He's still wearing his suit.'

'We didn't try to undress him, Colonel. Except for his shoes. We took those off, loosened his tie, covered him up and made him as comfortable as we could. It's what we always used to do with him. He went straight off to sleep. I thought he was still asleep in bed when I banged on his door this morning.'

'You didn't look to see?'

'No. I thought it was best to leave him. Maybe he woke up while we were at church this morning and took the boat out then?'

'I'd say he'd been in the water for longer than that.'

Geoffrey said, 'We'll go and call for an ambulance and phone the police as well. I think that's the drill. Will you stay here, Hugh?'

'Of course.'

He waited with the crew. They seemed badly shaken. The bomb aimer, Jack, kept shaking his head.

'Poor old Don. First rate when he was sober but a real cretin when he wasn't. He gets through the war without a scratch and then goes and does a stupid thing like this. Poor old Don.'

Nobody, it seemed, had heard the Australian making his way downstairs and out of the house during the night but that's what must have happened, the Colonel decided. The Cheethams always left the hall and landing lights on and the moon would have guided the man across the lawn to the lake and the jetty where the dinghy was moored. Untying the boat and getting into it must have been tricky in his state, and he had already demonstrated how useless he was at rowing. Falling overboard had been almost inevitable.

'Could he swim?'

'He was the only one of us who could,' Jim Harper said. 'He grew up by a beach in Sydney and we used to joke about him having the best chance if we ever came down in the sea. But the rest of us never learned as kids. It was all different before the war.'

That was true enough, the Colonel thought. Public swimming pools in England would have been relatively few, private ones only for the rich and privileged, and ordinary people didn't fly off on sunny summer holidays to foreign beaches. Today it was unusual for someone not to be able to swim, but not in those days.

He walked over to where the boat was caught up in the reeds, the oars floating some way out on the water. The thick mud on the lake bottom had sucked hard at his feet when he had plunged in to reach the body and it had been very difficult to make headway. The Australian might have been able to swim but he was drunk and a drunk man didn't need to be out of his depth to drown. All he needed was to be incapacitated.

The ambulance arrived with paramedics and when they had satisfied themselves that there was nothing more to be done for Don Wilson, they took him away. The crew watched the stretcher being loaded into the ambulance, standing together in a silent, stricken group. The Colonel went to change out of his wet clothes.

The police arrived an hour later – a young inspector with an even younger sergeant, following three respectful paces behind him. Inspector Dryden and Sergeant Reed.

The inspector's face was expressionless. 'Perhaps you could tell us what happened, Mr Cheetham.'

'We don't know exactly. Mr Wilson was attending the RAF Buckby Reunion over the weekend and staying with us here at The Grange.'

'He was a paying bed and breakfast guest?'

'Yes. We'd never met him before. He went to the reunion dinner in Lincoln yesterday evening where he drank rather a lot and was brought back here. At some time during the night we think he must have taken our dinghy out on to the lake by himself and fallen in.'

'Who brought him back from the dinner?'

'These six gentlemen. They were all members of the same Lancaster bomber crew during the war and Mr Wilson was their mid-upper gunner. He arrived unexpectedly from Australia on Friday evening.'

Bill Steed said, 'We hadn't seen or heard from Don for years, Inspector. We'd no idea that he was coming. Or that he'd be staying here.'

'And Mr Wilson drank a lot during the evening?'

'Yes. He was making a bit of a nuisance of himself so we took him away and brought him back here.'

'In what way was he making a nuisance of himself?'

'Talking nonsense, creating a rather embarrassing scene.'

'So you took him off?'

'That's right.'

'All six of you?'

'Yes. We'd been used to coping with him when he'd had one over the eight in the old days. We did thirty ops together, you see. We always looked after each other. Old habits die hard.'

'I understand, sir.'

How could the young inspector possibly understand, the Colonel wondered? How could he possibly comprehend the strength of the bond that held a bomber crew together? The unique brotherhood.

The inspector continued. 'What time did you get back with Mr Wilson?'

'Around ten.'

'And what happened then?'

'There was a very bright moon and Don wanted us all to go off for a row on the lake, like we'd done earlier that afternoon. Of course, we put a stop to the idea. We took him indoors and got him up the stairs to his room.'

'With difficulty?'

'He was quite drunk. Yes, it was difficult.'

'And then, sir?'

'We laid him on the bed, loosened his tie, removed his shoes and put the cover over him. Just like we used to do in the war whenever he'd had too much. He went out like a light – or so we thought – and we left him and went to bed ourselves. He must have woken up some time during the night and gone out to the lake. He'd do stupid things when he'd been drinking.'

'People do, sir. All too often. Didn't you check his room when he hadn't appeared for breakfast in the morning?'

'I knocked on his door but he didn't answer. We decided it was better to leave him to sleep. He'd had a long flight from Australia, as well as everything else, and he wasn't in very good shape. Not at his age.'

'Was the house front door locked last night, Mr Cheetham?'

'Yes, but it can be opened easily from the inside. We have it like that so that guests can get out quickly if there's a fire. We take our guests' safety seriously, Inspector.'

'I'm sure you do, sir. But the fact is that one of them has died. Was the boat easily accessible and left unattended?'

'It's kept moored at the jetty.'

'Do you have any warning notice displayed there?'

'Warning notice? No, we don't.'

'Boats and water constitute a hazard, Mr Cheetham. Paying guests should have their attention drawn to any possible risks. And there should be a lifebelt to hand.'

'We weren't aware that was necessary either.'

'It's in your interests, as well as in the guests'.'

There was a pause. The sergeant was writing notes busily.

'So, what will happen now, Inspector?'

'That's up to the coroner, Mr Cheetham. He or she may decide a post-mortem is required to verify the cause of death.'

'The man fell in the lake when he was drunk, and he drowned. Surely that's obvious enough? It was an accident.'

'It has to be established for certain, sir. And there remains the question of responsibility.'

'What do you mean – responsibility?'

'Whether any person or persons can be held responsible for Mr Wilson's death.'

'I don't see how anyone could be. He was alone.'

'We don't know that for sure yet, sir. When exactly did you and Mrs Cheetham return from the dinner?'

'Not until nearly midnight. The Colonel here is an old friend of mine staying with us as a private guest for the weekend and he drove us back in his car. Everyone else had already gone to bed. My wife went straight upstairs and the Colonel and I had a quick nightcap before we went too. It had been a long day. We were all tired.'

'Did you hear Mr Wilson going downstairs during the night?'

'No, we didn't. But we wouldn't have heard him unless he had made a lot of noise. My wife and I sleep at the front of the house away from the stairs. The Colonel's room is there too.'

'Overlooking the lake?'

'No, the lake is at the other end of the house.'

'How about the other bedrooms?'

'They're down another corridor, also away from the staircase. Nobody heard him.'

'What time do you get up in the morning, Mr Cheetham?'

'My wife and I are always up by six thirty when we have a full house. We have to get things ready for the breakfasts.'

'Can you see the lake from the kitchen?'

'Part of it, yes.'

'But not all of it?'

'No. Not all of it. There's a bend in the middle. And we certainly didn't see or hear Mr Wilson this morning, or last night either. Of course, Miss Warner's room is near the stairs. She might have heard him.'

'Miss Warner?'

'Another of our guests.'

'Is she also attending the RAF reunion?'

The Colonel waited with interest for Miss Warner to be explained to the inspector.

'No. She's taking part in the annual Tudor re-enactment up at the Hall. It's an annual three-week summer event.'

'Was she here last night?'

'Yes. She always has her supper on a tray in her room and my wife took it up to her before we left for the dinner in Lincoln. Miss Warner likes to retire very early. I imagine she sleeps soundly but I suppose it's possible that she heard something.'

'When will she be back?'

'Not usually until after five.'

'I'd like to speak to her as soon as she returns.'

Which would be even more interesting, the Colonel thought.

The inspector turned to him.

'Colonel, I understand it was you who discovered Mr Wilson's body in the lake and brought it out. What time was that?'

'About a quarter to one. I'd walked back to the house soon after the memorial church service had ended and I went down to the lake.'

'Any particular reason?'

'No. I was simply waiting for the others to come back from church. Passing the time. Mr and Mrs Cheetham's dog came with me and started barking at something round the corner of the bank. When I went to see what it was, I thought at first that it was some half-submerged rags among the weed. Then I saw the arms and hands and I realized it was a body, floating face down. The empty boat was caught up in the reeds by the bank and the oars some distance away.'

'And you brought the body out of the water immediately and tried to revive Mr Wilson?'

'I tried to, but unfortunately it was too late.'

'Mrs Cheetham, I take it that you have Mr Wilson's address in Australia? From when he made his booking with you?'

'I'm sorry but I don't. He phoned and I never learned his home address.'

'You didn't ask for it – for your records?'

She shook her head, distressed. 'I usually do, but it was a last-minute booking. He phoned from a public phone and it was a very short call.'

'I'd like to see his room, please, madam.'

Geoffrey said, 'I wonder, if you'd mind showing the inspector, Hugh?

'Not at all.'

The Colonel had no idea which attic room had been used by the Australian but when he opened the first door at the top of the stairs it turned out to be a lucky guess. The bed cover was thrown back, the sheet creased and the pillow still held the imprint of Don Wilson's head. His shoes had been put neatly beside the bed. Without thinking, the Colonel picked one up. It was scuffed and unpolished with worn-down heels, and it felt damp.

'If you don't mind, sir . . .'

He replaced it at once.

'I wonder why he didn't put his shoes on before he went out.'

'Would you have bothered, sir? If you'd been drinking a lot?'

'No, I imagine not.'

He watched while the two policemen went over the room, opening the shabby suitcase on the luggage rack, searching through the contents of the sponge bag in the adjoining bathroom, opening and shutting drawers and the wardrobe. There was very little to see. The suitcase held only a few basic clothes, the wardrobe nothing at all. There were no photographs, no address book or diary, no paperbacks or magazines and no wallet, which would probably be in a pocket of the suit Don Wilson was wearing when he drowned. The only other possession belonging to the dead man was his chrome watch lying on the bedside table – evidently removed by the crew, along with the shoes, though they hadn't mentioned it.

'I see they took his watch off.'

'So they did, sir.'

It had been placed on its edge so that Wilson would be able to see the dial when he woke up. A nice, considerate touch, the Colonel thought. He bent to take a closer look. Nothing special about it. Just a cheap chrome model like millions of others, but it happened to be showing exactly the right time.

The inspector closed the wardrobe door with a shrug. He seemed to take a dim view of drunk-drownings.

'They usually happen in a private swimming pool, sir. You'd be amazed how careless some people are about basic safety rules, specially at parties. Alcohol's nearly always the key factor. I don't have much sympathy with the adults, to tell the truth. That's their look out. It's the kids I care about – the little ones left unsupervised near a pool. Parents too busy or enjoying themselves too much to keep a proper eye on them. Drowning only takes a few minutes, that's the tragedy. Did you know Mr Wilson well, sir?'

'I didn't know him at all. I first met him when he arrived here late on Friday evening. We only spoke a few times.'

'What sort of impression did he make on you?'

'It's rather hard to say on such a short acquaintance. He told me that when he went back to Australia after the war was over he couldn't settle down. He was something of a rolling stone, I gathered. Odd labouring jobs in Queensland, married and divorced twice . . . He said he won some money recently on the horses and used it to buy an airline ticket to come over for the RAF reunion.'

'He and his old crew seem to have been great buddies.'

'They certainly would have been during the war. They hadn't seen him for many years but the bond was still there, as you will have noticed, inspector.'

Another shrug. No, he obviously hadn't understood at all. How could he?

'Well, the Australian police should be able to help us find out more about him and whether he has any family left Down Under.'

They were going down the stairs when Miss Warner, in Tudor guise, entered through the front door, right on cue. The inspector might be very capable at handling most eventualities but the Colonel felt that this time he might be about to meet his match.

TEN

The policemen went away, taking the Australian's meagre possessions with them.

As the Colonel had anticipated, the inspector had had a sticky time with Miss Warner. She had approached the staircase as they were descending and stopped dead, a hand clasped to her bosom.

'But stay! Who comes here?'

The Colonel had enlightened her as to who did come there and, to help things along, he had also explained briefly what had happened. Miss Warner had looked distressed – far more than necessary since she had hardly set eyes on the Australian. All the re-enacting was bound to take over.

'What ill news is this! Poor gentleman! Woe is me!'

The inspector had hesitated, but only for a second. 'I understand you retired to your room early yesterday, Miss Warner?'

''Tis my custom.'

'And did you go to sleep early?'

'I did. I was sore weary.'

'Mr Wilson was brought back early from a dinner in Lincoln by the six gentlemen also staying here. Did you happen to hear them helping him up the stairs to his room?'

'Indeed I did, sir. They didst wake me with all the commotion they made. Methinks, Mr Wilson had drunk deep, if I am not mistook.'

The inspector took a slow breath. 'Miss Warner, I must ask you to speak in plain English.'

'Marry, I do not understand you, sir. My tongue is as plain as yours and in truth I can speak no other.'

Another deep breath. 'Miss Warner, please answer this

question clearly. Did you hear Mr Wilson coming down the stairs later on, at any time during the night or in the early hours of this morning?'

'Verily, I did not. The arms of Morpheus had reclaimed me and I heard naught.'

The inspector had finally conceded defeat.

'This is a terrible business, Hugh. It's upset Heather very badly. She feels we're responsible, which is rubbish, of course. It was an accident, pure and simple.'

'I'm very sorry it should have happened, Geoffrey.'

'Would you have a word with her, Hugh? I'm sure you'd be able to calm things down. You always talk good sense. People listen to you.'

He was always being told so, but he couldn't imagine why. For some reason, people believed that he would know the best thing to do in difficult circumstances. Usually, he had no more idea than they did.

He found Heather in the kitchen, washing up.

'Can I give you a hand?'

'No thanks, Hugh.'

'I'm quite good at drying.'

She turned round and he saw the tears in her eyes.

'I'm awfully sorry to be so feeble, Hugh, but it's such a dreadful thing to have happened. Really horrible!'

'It's certainly very unfortunate, but it wasn't your fault. And you mustn't take it to heart.'

'But you heard what the inspector said – we should have put a warning notice up at the jetty.'

He said firmly, 'If you'd put ten notices there, Heather, it wouldn't have made any difference. The man was drunk. He'd made up his mind that he wanted to go for a row in the moonlight and nothing was going to stop him. If it's anyone's fault, it's his own.'

She fumbled for a handkerchief in the pocket of her apron and wiped her eyes.

'We'll probably get the blame for it, though. And we'll lose our reputation and all our customers.'

'Why would you do that?'

'Who'd want to come and stay now? After someone has died here?'

He said, 'How old is The Grange, Heather?'

She stared at him. 'What do you mean?'

'How old is the house?'

'About two hundred years or more.'

'And how many people do you think must have died here during that time?'

'I've no idea. I've never really thought about it.'

'Well, I dare say it would add up to quite a number. The old man who lived in my cottage before me died upstairs in bed in the room where I sleep now; so did his wife. And heaven knows how many before them. People die upstairs and downstairs in houses, indoors and outdoors. It happens all the time.'

'The local paper's bound to report it.'

'If they do, it'll be forgotten in a week. He was a stranger from twelve thousand miles away.'

'But he was a war hero, too, wasn't he?'

'One of many who attended the reunion.'

She twisted the handkerchief in her hands. 'The thing is, Hugh, I've been thinking about the future anyway. We really ought to give up doing B&B. Sell The Grange and move somewhere much smaller and more manageable.'

'Do you really want to do that?'

'No. But it's not fair on Geoffrey to stay here. He could be having a nice, peaceful retirement with no work or worries. Instead, he's slaving away and spending money on a crumbling old pile that will never make much profit. We just about break even, that's all. There's no point, is there?'

He said slowly, 'I think there's a great deal of point. Doing nothing when you retire is definitely a bad idea. If you don't keep busy you can lose your grip on life. The Grange is very good for Geoffrey. It would be a mistake to throw in the towel. And, in any case, he wouldn't want to leave the old airfield now, would he? He's become very much involved with it. Very attached.'

'I know. But it seems such a sad place to me.'

'He sees it differently.'

'But I always think about all those young men dying. The terrible waste.'

'You mustn't look at it in that way, Heather. They died for something worth fighting and dying for. That's not always the case in wars, believe me.'

As the Colonel left the kitchen, Bill Steed came down the stairs, carrying a suitcase.

'We'll be off soon, Colonel. No sense in us hanging around any longer. The inspector said they'd keep us notified about arrangements for Don's funeral. They'll be getting in touch with his family in Australia – that's if he has any to find. Two ex-wives and no children, Don told us. He never mentioned any brothers or sisters or any other relatives that we can remember.'

'I'm sorry that your weekend should have ended like this.'

'Yes, we're feeling very bad indeed about it. We should have looked after him better.'

'He wasn't actually your responsibility.'

'Yes, he was. Once a bomber crew, always a bomber crew. It's for life. People don't always appreciate that. We chose each other at the start, you know.'

The Colonel nodded. 'Rather shrewd of the RAF to let you all pick your own destiny.'

'Yes, it makes for strong ties.'

The rest of the crew came down the stairs with their luggage and Geoffrey and Heather appeared to see them off. The Colonel was included in the goodbyes.

'Very pleased to have met you, Colonel,' Jim Harper, the navigator said, shaking his hand. 'And thank you for what you did for Don.'

'I wish I had been able to save him.'

'You did everything you could. It's us who let him down. We feel like we've lost a brother.'

He had spoken quietly and without overt emotion, but then death would be no stranger to him, the Colonel thought. Nor to any of them.

Someone had laid a bunch of flowers by The Grange gatepost. As the cars drove off, Geoffrey went to pick them up. They were brightly coloured and wrapped in shiny plastic. He looked at them with distaste.

'I don't understand why people do this sort of thing for someone they never knew or met, do you?'

Heather said, 'Just throw them away, please Geoffrey.' She hurried back into the house.

He went on staring down at the flowers. 'They must be sick, Hugh. I could just about understand it when the Princess of Wales died – I suppose people felt they knew her, even if they didn't. But it's become a sort of gruesome ritual now, hasn't it? Everyone wants to join in the mourning. God knows why.'

'If I were you, I'd do what Heather asked. Throw them away before they encourage any more.'

'Good advice, as always. I hope you'll stay on for a few days, Hugh. We'd be glad of your company. Moral support and all that . . . until we know how things are going to turn out.'

He thought of Thursday locked up in Cat Heaven. Five-star accommodation it might be, but as far as a footloose stray was concerned, it was still a prison. He would be sulking furiously and maybe refusing to eat, no matter what delicacies were placed before him. If Thursday had considered himself betrayed when he had been left behind at the cottage once before, the Colonel might find he had completely overstepped the mark this time. He might do a lot more than sulk; he might move on.

He said, 'I'd need to make a phone call.'

Mrs Moffat answered the Cat Heaven telephone.

'Thursday is quite all right, Colonel. He was a little bit upset at first but now he's settled in very well.'

She would say that, he thought.

'Is he eating?'

'Oh yes. Fish is his favourite, as you probably know. Especially pilchards. He's very friendly, isn't he? We have a little chat every morning and evening and he lets me give him a nice brush and comb. Not every cat will do that, I can tell you.'

She must have muddled the names up, he decided. It would be easy enough, with all those cats. He'd never had such a thing as a little chat with Thursday – merely a brief word or two – and the idea of a nice brush and comb being permitted was unthinkable.

He said uncertainly. 'That doesn't sound very much like Thursday. He's the old black and tan moggie with the torn ear.'

'Yes, that's the one. I assure you I know *all* my boarders, Colonel. And I make a particular point of them getting to know me. It's all about trust, you see. A trusting cat is a contented cat, I always say. You're collecting him tomorrow, aren't you?'

He said, 'I wondered if perhaps you could keep him for a day or two longer?'

'I'm usually chock-a-block at this time of year, Colonel, but there's been an unexpected cancellation, so that would be perfectly all right.'

He rang Naomi next.

'Just thought I should let you know that I've been asked to stay on here for a bit.'

She cackled; there was no better word to describe the sound that came down the wire. A loud cackle.

'Another woman after you, Hugh?'

'Of course not.'

'Found another body, then?'

'What do you mean?'

'Well, you keep bumping into them. First it was Ursula Swynford suffocated at the Manor fête, then that actress you found electrocuted in her bath, and last time it was a Swedish girl's skeleton you dug up in your friend's barn.'

'The builders dug her up, not me.'

'Same result. You had to hang around, trying to sort things out. So, whose body is it this time?'

He said stiffly, 'As a matter of fact, one of the B and B guests drowned in a boating accident on the lake here.'

'Another woman?'

'No, a man.'

'That makes a change.'

'An Australian.'

'You'd think he could swim, being an Aussie.'

'He could swim, but he was drunk.'

'Well, they usually are in my experience.'

Naomi's experience of Antipodeans, so far as he knew, was limited to one visit to stay with her son and Australian daughter-in-law in a very respectable part of Brisbane. And, unlike Naomi herself, her daughter-in-law never touched a drop.

He said, 'Anyway, it's all been very unfortunate.'

'Did you meet the body – before it drowned?'

'Yes. He'd come over to attend a Bomber Command Reunion. His old crew were staying here too.'

'They must have been a bit upset.'

'Very.'

'The uncle I told you about flew in Lancasters. He always said his crew were like brothers to him. In fact, he said he knew them better than his own real brothers. And liked them a lot better.'

He thought of Jim Harper's sad remark.

'I imagine that was often the case.'

'I'll tell you another thing about my uncle. After the war was over, he never had to buy himself another pint again. He was the local hero for the rest of his life.'

'The crews at the reunion were treated like that. Everyone made a big fuss of them.'

'And so they should. They deserved it. By the way, what about Thursday?'

'I rang the cattery. The woman who runs it said she'll keep him a bit longer. She said he's perfectly all right.'

'Cats aren't stupid. They know how to look after themselves.'

That might well be said of Thursday, but nonetheless the Colonel felt that the cosying-up to Mrs Moffat was inexplicable.

'I'll go round and water anything that's looking thirsty, Hugh. Don't worry.'

'Very kind of you, Naomi.'

'Shall I get Jacob to give the grass a once-over?'

He said firmly, 'No, thank you.'

For Jacob to give the grass a once-over meant getting out the lawn mower, which meant unlocking the shed, which meant revealing to Naomi his new hiding place for the keys as well as giving her the perfect pretext to invade his sanctum in his absence.

'I wouldn't leave it too long, if I were you. Not good for it.'

'Don't worry, I'll be back in a day or two.'

'You might find out that the drowning wasn't an accident, after all.'

'That's not very likely, Naomi. It's cut and dried.'

'It never seems to be when you're around.'

Afterwards, he walked down to the lake and on to the jetty where the dinghy had been moored again, the oars retrieved and stowed away. Cut and dried, he had told Naomi. But it wasn't quite so simple as that, was it? Not when he thought more about it. The boat was the old-fashioned clinker-built wooden sort, not made of flimsy lightweight modern plastic. It was solid and sturdy. The whole crew had squashed into it that afternoon when he and Geoffrey had watched from the bank. Seven old men larking about like kids. They'd shipped some water, rocking it, true enough, but the overloaded dinghy had stayed steady. That night Don Wilson had been on his own and he ought to have been safe enough. Except, of course, that he was drunk. And drunk men do stupid things like losing both oars and then leaning over, trying to retrieve them. And falling into water blanketed with thick weed and with a mud bottom like a quagmire.

Geoffrey said, 'That confounded local reporter's turned up, Hugh. Would you get rid of him for us? Heather's been upset enough.'

The young man was waiting in the hall, notebook in hand.

The Colonel said pleasantly, 'Mr Cheetham would be grateful if you'd leave. Neither he, nor Mrs Cheetham, has anything to say.'

'I understand, sir. They must be very distressed by the accident. But my editor still wants this article: "Forgotten Heroes." And he thinks it would be a good touch to put in something special about Mr Wilson . . . some sort of tribute to the part he played in the war. Coming all that way from Australia to fight on our side, and so on. He thinks it would go down rather well.'

'I agree, but Mr and Mrs Cheetham only met Mr Wilson when he arrived here on Friday evening. They know almost nothing about him.'

'Would you yourself have any information, sir? He might have talked to you?'

He was a decent young man and a reporter's job was to dig for lumps of gold or for any possible dirt.

'No, I'm afraid I can't help you. We hardly spoke.'

'He had some rather interesting things to say about Bomber Command at the dinner in Lincoln. When they were serving the drinks before.'

'Such as?'

'He said that serving as crew was a mug's game.'

'I expect he'd already had a glass or two.'

'He seemed quite sober then. He said most of them didn't have a chance but that the RAF didn't give a damn. It didn't matter how many of them were killed because there were always plenty of other mugs to take their place. Of course, he got pretty drunk during the dinner later on and finally those other old guys came up and hauled him away. I only realized they were his former crew when you pointed them out to me later, after the church service yesterday. It was nice the way they took care of him.'

'It's the custom, I believe.'

'They clammed-up completely when I spoke to them at the church. A lot of the veterans are like that though; you'd never guess they'd done a thing in the war. Won't say a word.'

Unlike Naomi's uncle and his free pints, the Colonel thought. He knew that it was not uncommon for people who had suffered a very grim war to keep silent about it, even with their families. Some would reveal things at the very end of their lives, perhaps to their grandchildren; others would take their story to the grave.

He said, 'That creepback business you mentioned. Did you ask them about it?'

'Yes, I did. They'd never heard of it.'

But they *must* have done, the Colonel thought. According to the Air Vice-Marshal, it was a known phenomenon of the time: bombs falling further and further short of the target as a long raid went on. And if their mid-upper gunner had known about it, so had they. Still, the Colonel could quite see why the crew had closed ranks against a cocky young reporter with his notebook and his nosy questions.

'I'm sorry I can't be of any help to you. Good luck with your article.'

'Of course, I can't repeat what he said about it being a mug's game. Not in this article. Are you sure there's nothing he told you that I could use?'

He felt rather sorry for the young chap; he seemed genuine enough and the article was a very good idea. And it was right that there should be something written in praise of the Australian gunner.

'Well, he told me how they crewed up. It was rather interesting. I think your readers would enjoy hearing about it.'

The notepad reappeared in a flash.

'What did he say?'

'I'll tell you, if you guarantee that there will be no mention in your article of Mr Wilson staying here at The Grange and no photograph of the house.'

If the local grapevine was anything like the one in Frog End then everyone would know anyway, but at least it might comfort Heather not to have her old home feature on the front page.

'Not a word, Colonel.'

'And no photo of the house?'

'Not one.' The pencil hovered. 'How did they do it?'

'Not like you'd imagine at all.'

ELEVEN

There were no Bed & Breakfast bookings until the following weekend and the Colonel made himself generally useful. He fed the rescued hens who were already looking brighter and better and bolder, and watched them pecking and scratching and fluffing out their growing feathers. They were even beginning to lay eggs and collecting them warm from the nesting boxes was a new experience for him; he had only known them cold and old in cardboard boxes off shop shelves.

He mowed the lawns, raked the gravel and helped Geoffrey make yet another assault on the blanket weed. It was, he realized, a hopeless cause – Heather had already told him so, based on her long experience of the lake. But the attempt had to be made. Their ammunition was a new brand killer guaranteeing miraculous results. It came in plastic bags which could be thrown into the water where the bag dissolved, releasing (according to makers) a trillion freeze dried bacteria, harmless to all fauna, fish and flora – except the blanket weed.

They divided the bags and the lake between them. Geoffrey to cover the outer section in his chest-high waders, the Colonel to deal with the centre from the dinghy. He had done a fair bit of rowing at school and in the army and the boat was very easy to handle. He rowed backwards and forwards, dropping bags at the correct distance from each other. From time to time, fish broke the surface of the water and he knew that they were following him to and fro – curious, or hungry, or both. Several times, he caught sight of the ghost carp.

*　　*　　*

The inspector phoned later. Geoffrey took the call and came out on to the terrace where the Colonel was sitting with Heather.

'They've done a post-mortem. Death by drowning and he was awash with alcohol. Nothing suspicious and no inquest necessary, thank God. The body's been released for burial but the Australian police can't trace any family over there, except for two ex-wives who didn't want to know anything about him. No children or other relations. Poor fellow, it's all rather sad. And there's only a few dollars in his bank account, so the problem is who pays the burial expenses and where is he to be buried? Not much point sending him all the way back to Australia, in the circumstances. I told the inspector I'd have a word with the vicar here and the local branch of the RAF Association. See if something decent could be worked out. I reckon he deserves it.'

'His crew will want to know,' Heather said. 'They were like brothers.'

'Good morning, Colonel. Another beautiful day.'

She had used perfectly normal speech and she was wearing perfectly normal clothes: a plain skirt, blouse and cardigan such as English women of a certain age and type frequently wear. He rather expected her to be eating a plain boiled or poached egg but she was tackling the Full English with the usual gusto.

'Good morning, Miss Warner.'

He fetched some cornflakes and sat down at the table. She passed him the jug of milk and the sugar.

'I'm leaving today, as you see, Colonel. Sadly, I have to return to the real world.'

'I hope you've enjoyed your stay.'

He didn't know quite what else to call it; holiday was hardly the right word when she had been slaving away, baking bread from morning till night while the gentry loafed about.

'I always do. I take part in the re-enactment every year.'

'Then you must enjoy it very much.'

'It makes such a change from my other life, you see.'

'Which is?'

'I work for my local council. In the Refuse and Recycling Department. Very little romance there.'

He smiled. 'I suppose not.'

'For three weeks I escape into another world. The world of four hundred years ago. It's the best kind of holiday I know and I can thoroughly recommend it. So much better than a cruise. There are still some places available for next year, if you're interested.'

He wondered exactly what role she had in mind for him. If he could choose, he thought that he would settle for being a gallant knight in armour, galloping around on horseback, re-fighting some ancient battle with clashing swords. He certainly wouldn't want to be one of the gentry, sitting around doing nothing all day.

As though she were following his thoughts, she said, 'They're definitely doing Bosworth. It's all decided.'

'That's an interesting choice.'

'You could ride with the king as one of his loyal personal guard – knights of the body, they were called. Poor Richard! Dragged from his noble horse, White Surrey, as he led the charge against Henry Tudor and brutally hacked to death. A dreadful end and his body shamefully treated afterwards. He was the last of our kings to die in battle, you know.'

'Yes, I did know. If you don't count James IV at Flodden thirty years or so later.'

'Which I don't. He wasn't English.'

This was irrefutable. The Scottish king, cut down on the Northumberland fields of Flodden with his nobles and ten thousand troops was dismissed as of little consequence as Miss Warner warmed to her theme.

'Come to that, Richard was the last *English* king of all. After him they were all foreigners. Welsh, Scots, Dutch,

German . . . every sort. Much as I admire the Tudors, the Plantagenets definitely had the edge when it came to breeding. No one can fault their lineage. They thought the world of Richard in the North, you know. And all that nonsense about him having a hunch back and a withered arm was made up by Shakespeare. It was all Tudor propaganda.'

In a moment, he feared, they would be on to the conundrum of the Princes in the Tower but, instead, Miss Warner started buttering her toast.

'Will you be staying here long, Colonel?'

'Just a day or two.'

'Well, I'm sure Mr and Mrs Cheetham will be glad of your company until the dust has settled over the accident. Such a dreadful thing to happen. Mr Wilson must have drunk far too much but then Australians often do, don't they?'

Naomi would have agreed.

'You said they made rather a lot of noise taking him upstairs to bed that evening, Miss Warner – when you were woken up.'

'Oh yes. An unnecessary amount, I thought.'

'Unnecessary?'

'Quite unnecessary. Banging about and swearing loudly at the poor man. They didn't seem the kind of gentlemen who would normally swear but I suppose they were fed up with him by then. He must have spoiled their evening.'

'I've no doubt he swore back.'

'I didn't hear him. I should think he was beyond it. Anyway, they were much quieter when they came down. They tiptoed past my room.'

'And you didn't hear anything later on? Mr Wilson coming downstairs again?'

'Not a sound. As I told that inspector, I went back to sleep quite quickly. Whatever can have got into his head to make him do such a silly thing?'

'I've no idea.'

Perhaps it had been the bomber's moon? The impulse to do something reckless? The urge to retrieve his lost youth? To rediscover the big adventure of his life? The one part he could be proud of? The one part that had not been a failure?

Miss Warner was spooning some of the home-made marmalade on to her side plate. 'Of course, they would have taken his shoes off when they put him to bed, wouldn't they? So he wouldn't have made much noise when he came down.'

He remembered the pair of shoes placed at the foot of the bed. The one he had picked up had felt damp but there was a simple enough explanation for that. There had been no other shoes in his luggage. The Australian would have been wearing the same pair as he had worn for the afternoon's unsteady jaunt on the lake when they'd shipped a fair amount of water.

Miss Warner spread the marmalade. 'I suppose he'll be taken back to Australia.'

'He doesn't seem to have any family there. I gather it's possible that he might be buried here in Buckby, if it can be arranged.'

'That sounds like a very good idea. A suitable resting place for a man who came halfway round the world to fight for this country in her hour of need. Don't you agree, Colonel?'

'Yes, I do,' he said. 'Completely.'

She put down her knife. 'He was different from the rest of his crew, quite apart from being Australian. I only saw him once and we never spoke but I'm very observant about people. He was the odd man out. Did you notice?'

The seventh link, he thought. Not necessarily the weakest but, yes, definitely different.

Miss Warner left after breakfast and he said goodbye to her in the hall.

'I shall hope to see you at the re-enactment next year, Colonel.'

It would be uncivil to dash her hopes and untrue to raise them. He chose the middle way.

'Possibly, Miss Warner.'

She considered him, her head tilted to one side.

'You'd make a very good knight.'

TWELVE

Don Wilson, former mid-upper gunner of a World War Two Lancaster crew, was buried with ceremony in the churchyard of St Luke's, Buckby, a few days later.

It was impressive to see how the vicar, the RAF Association, the RAF Benevolent Fund and the villagers had all worked together to give him a dignified farewell. The church was full and after the service, the coffin, draped in the Australian flag, was carried out on the shoulders of young servicemen and followed slowly by the six surviving members of his old crew. Two RAF buglers played the Last Post when the coffin had been lowered into the grave.

All properly done, the Colonel thought, and very moving. Due respect paid. A decent conclusion to what seemed to have been rather a wretched life. Even his courageous war service had not, apparently, given the Australian much personal satisfaction. He remembered their conversation: *I've plenty to remember and none of it good . . .*

People began to drift away and he went over to speak to the crew who were, in effect, the chief mourners. They had driven up for the burial and though Heather had invited them to stay the night at The Grange they had told her that they would drive back immediately afterwards. It seemed just as well in the circumstances.

'It's all been a bit of a blow,' Davies, the bomb aimer, said. 'Poor old Don. The first one of us to go.'

As you grew older, the Colonel reflected, all funerals were unsettling reminders of your own mortality. This particular one would have been especially so for these men.

'He's in a good place.'

'That's true. And we're grateful for that.'

The Colonel murmured a few words to the rest of the crew who scarcely responded.

The skipper said to him, 'We never thought this would happen. It takes some getting used to.'

'I'm sure.'

'We went through a lot together. The seven of us.'

The Colonel said sympathetically, 'You must have done.'

'We didn't meet for years after but things won't be the same now that he's gone. If you can understand that.'

'Yes, I think I can.'

'Don talked to you, didn't he? Did he say much about the war?'

The Colonel hesitated. 'Well, he said he'd got a lot to remember and none of it was good. I'm not sure exactly what he meant by that.'

'It depends on how you look at things, I suppose. He always had his own point of view. He could be a difficult customer.'

'So it would seem. Apparently, he told the local newspaper reporter that serving as crew in Bomber Command was a mug's game. That the RAF didn't care about the losses because the men could easily be replaced.'

'Just the sort of thing he would say, I'm afraid. I hope the reporter didn't take him seriously.'

'I don't think so. His article is about heroes. Nothing contentious.'

'That's a relief.'

Others came up and soon the crew were surrounded by people wanting to shake their hands. Six elderly men, still quiet and unassuming in spite of all the admiring attention being paid to them.

The Colonel moved away.

The newspaper reporter appeared.

'The article will be in tomorrow, Colonel.'

'I'll be sure to look out for it.'

'The title's been changed to: "Unsung Heroes."'

'That sounds much better.'

'There'll probably be a shot of the RAF buglers today. It will make the point rather well, don't you think? The present honouring the past.'

'Perfectly.'

'He was rather a rum customer, the Aussie, wasn't he?'

Bill Steed had called him a difficult one; the reporter saw him as rum. It was much the same.

'What makes you say that?'

'Well, I've just been talking to a young guy who met him at the reunion dinner. He's been telling me about it.'

'Oh?'

'Apparently, the Aussie insisted that he and his crew weren't heroes at all. Anything *but* heroes, in fact. Just the opposite.'

'How so?'

'He said that they did the first two ops and found out just what hell it was. They also found out that they'd only got a one in three chance of surviving their tour. So, they decided to give themselves better odds.'

'How did they manage that?'

'By dropping their bombs short of the target and buzzing off home. That's what he said. They got away with it because nobody was expected to be perfect in the early days. It was all pretty chaotic and bombs got dropped all over the place, often nowhere near the target. On a real stinker of an op like Berlin, he said they'd pretend something was wrong so they could turn back. Hydraulics, magneto, oil pressure, R/T . . . whatever. Any excuse. With any luck, the next target they were given would be a safer one. Or, if it wasn't, they'd dump their bombs in the sea. That was the general idea, he said. Making things easy for themselves. They'd got it all worked out together. Of course, this guy listening to him was shocked rigid until he finally cottoned on that he was having his leg pulled. It was all a

big joke. The Aussie was just kidding.' The reporter grinned.
'It wouldn't have gone down too well in my piece on
heroes, would it?'

Creepback, the Colonel thought. Creepback. But not
the involuntary tendency during long raids as described
by the Air Vice-Marshal. Don Wilson had meant something
else entirely. Deliberately unloading bombs too soon.
Deliberately turning back early. Calculated cowardice.
And he hadn't been joking.

After a while, the crew drove away amid salutes and
waves. Skipper, flight engineer, navigator, bomb aimer,
wireless operator, rear gunner, leaving their mid-upper
gunner behind. The Colonel watched them go. He wondered
if they would ever return to visit his grave. Somehow he
doubted it.

'Whisky, Hugh?'

'That would be good.'

Geoffrey poured two large measures.

'Damned shame it all had to end like that. Heather's still
really cut up about it.'

'Yes, I know.'

'I keep telling her it wasn't our fault. Nobody's blaming
us. It was an accident, for God's sake.'

'I'm sure she'll feel better about it in time.'

'She keeps saying we ought to sell The Grange and move
somewhere else. Give up the whole B and B thing.'

'Do you agree with her?'

'No, I don't, as a matter of fact. It has its drawbacks –
like Miss Warner – but it keeps me busy and out of mischief.
Besides, there's the old control tower to consider. We've
got plans to make it into a decent museum, did I tell you?
Collect old photos, memorabilia, uniforms, genuine fittings
and furniture – all that sort of thing. Quite a project. I
wouldn't want to miss out on it.'

'That sounds like a very good idea.'

'Can you stay on a few more days? I could show you what we've got in mind. Get your input.'

'It's kind of you, Geoffrey, but I ought to be getting back.'

'Well, stay until tomorrow at least.'

The local paper was delivered the next morning and the Colonel retrieved it from the front door mat. The reporter's article, headed 'Unsung Heroes', was on the front page. The Colonel skimmed through it . . .

> *This weekend saw the gathering of fifty-four heroes from the Second World War. Men now well into their eighties, who served at RAF Buckby and risked their lives night after night in the bombing campaign against Hitler's Nazi Germany. They assembled to remember the comrades they had lost in the struggle and to renew old acquaintance. For too long their vital contribution to victory has been ignored or even condemned by people, many of whom were not born until years afterwards and who have little or no understanding of what was at stake. But this weekend those men, and their comrades who died for our freedom, were given full acknowledgement. A fine stained glass window was unveiled in their honour in St Luke's church, Buckby, after a moving service of thanksgiving.*

There was a photograph of the memorial window, the group photograph taken at the dinner, and the separate photograph of Bill, Jim, Roger, Bob, Ben, Jack and Don, captioned: *Seven heroes: a Lancaster bomber crew reunited 57 years later.*

At the end there was a brief mention of the sad accidental death of the Australian mid-upper gunner, Don Wilson, with a picture of the RAF buglers at his burial at St Luke's. Nothing about The Grange, and no photo. The reporter had kept his word.

After breakfast, the Colonel took a final walk round the lake with Geoffrey.

His friend was frowning. 'Damned blanket weed. Worse than ever, if you ask me. That new stuff's useless.'

As usual, the fish had spotted their presence and a hungry escort followed their progress. Once or twice the Colonel caught the pale glint of the ghost carp. They passed the jetty where the dinghy was moored.

'Heather wants me to get rid of the boat.'

'It might be a good idea, if it upsets her.'

'But it's a nice old thing. I mean, look at it, Hugh. Steady as a rock. It was entirely that chap's own fault. He was a drunken fool.'

The Colonel agreed with the drunken part, but he didn't believe that Don Wilson had been a fool, whatever else he had been.

They walked away from the lake, past the rescued hens who had ventured bravely forth from their run and were enjoying a glorious freedom for the first time in their lives.

Geoffrey said, 'One last look at the old airfield?'

'Of course.'

He followed his friend through the gateway that led towards the perimeter track and the two of them stood at its edge, in silence for a moment.

The wind was making the ripe corn rattle sharply; short, dense, common market corn unlike the long-stalked, feathery old-fashioned kind of the Colonel's childhood that used to whisper softly.

He said, 'Did you know that Don Wilson told someone at the reunion dinner that he and his crew were anything but heroes?'

'He was drunk.'

'But he was quite insistent about it, apparently. He claimed that when they crewed up they agreed that they would do whatever they could to improve their chances of survival.'

'No harm in that.'

'No, of course not. But do you remember my asking you what creepback meant?'

'I've still no idea.'

'Well, the Air Vice-Marshal enlightened me after the memorial service. It was the term used by Bomber Command when crews dropped their bombs increasingly short of a target during a long raid – unintentionally, of course. But Don Wilson said his crew decided that's what they'd do – deliberately – so they could turn back sooner. They also decided that if they were given a particularly tough target they'd claim something was wrong with the plane and head for home early, gambling on an easier op the next time round. Sometimes they just dumped their bombs in the sea.'

'I don't believe a word of it, Hugh. Not a word.'

'It *is* hard to believe, I agree.'

'I grant you that there may have been the odd bomber crew not quite up to scratch, but the men we had staying here with us this weekend were first-class types. They'd never have done such a thing. It's unthinkable.'

'I'm sure you're right.'

'You saw what they were like.'

'Yes, indeed. Very impressive.'

'And you saw what the Aussie was like. Not at all impressive. I suppose it was his idea of a joke, and one in pretty poor taste, I might add. Did the rest of the crew know he was saying that sort of thing about them?'

'Well, I gather he was speaking out loud and clear. Perhaps that was the reason they took him away from the dinner.'

'Just as well they did. Somebody might have taken him seriously.'

The Colonel looked across the cornfield towards the old control tower, sentinel to the grim struggle. Death for so many. Survival only for the very lucky ones.

'Yes,' he agreed. 'They might.'

THIRTEEN

I t took some time for Mrs Moffat to answer his ring at the door of Cat Heaven. Time enough for the Colonel to picture what might await him. An emaciated and pitiful Thursday who had abandoned all hope of rescue? Who had turned his face to the wall and lost the will to live? A guilty prospect.

'There you are, Colonel . . . right on time.'

Actually, he was early. He had driven straight to the cattery before going to Pond Cottage.

'How is Thursday?'

'Oh, he's tip-top. He's been a perfect guest. Like I told you, we've formed quite a bond. Come and see for yourself.'

She unlocked the gate at the side of the house and they walked down the path to the cattery outbuilding. Mrs Moffat was in something emerald green and flowing, with the blonde beehive in such perfect order that he wondered if it was a wig. She looked totally unsuited to the daily grind of coping with other people's cats and yet she clearly was – chattering on gaily about the little talks and the brushing and combings. Another door was unlocked and he passed down the long row of cages and cats. A Siamese clawed desperately at the wire mesh emitting blood-curdling yowls.

'Here he is, bless him.'

Thursday was curled up asleep in a cushioned basket. Far from emaciated and sad, he looked perfectly content, well fed and certainly well brushed. The Colonel could not remember ever seeing his coat look so glossy.

'Hallo, old chap.'

Thursday lifted his head and stretched his front paws, unsheathing long, curved claws. He ignored the Colonel.

'I'll put him in his carrier for you, shall I? Then you can take him straight home.'

He waited humbly while Mrs Moffat scooped Thursday deftly into the carrier and fastened the door. She waggled her fingertips through the grille.

'I'm going to miss you, sweetheart . . . come and stay with me again soon.'

The Colonel put the carrier on the front passenger seat of the Riley. On the drive home, all he could see was Thursday's back turned towards him. No movement, no sign of recognition let alone rapprochement.

'I'm back, Naomi.'

'Jolly good!' Her voice barked at him down the wire.

'Thanks for keeping an eye on things.'

'Any time. I threw a bit of water over the terrace pots, that's all. Everything else has looked after itself. We had a jolly good downpour the other night.'

'I've just collected Thursday from Cat Heaven.'

'How is he?'

'Extraordinarily well. He seems to have got on with Mrs Moffat like a house on fire. They're bosom friends, apparently.'

'Well, cats aren't fools, Hugh. They know how to look after number one. They're cunning devils.'

'I'm in the doghouse, of course. He's gone off somewhere in a huff.'

'You would be. Don't worry, he'll come back all in good time.'

'How about a drink on the terrace, if it's not too late for you?'

'It's never too late, Hugh. I'll be round in twenty minutes.'

The phone rang as soon as he had replaced the receiver. It was his daughter-in-law, Susan, checking on his return.

'Are you all right, Father?'

'Perfectly, thank you.'

'It's always bit of a worry for us, when you go off.'

He knew that he should have been grateful that there was anyone to worry about him at all.

'How are you?'

'Eric's gone down with another cold and it's gone straight to his chest, of course.'

'I'm sorry to hear that.'

'Edith hasn't caught it yet, but I expect she will.'

'Marcus all right?'

'He's very stressed at the moment.'

Stress was the new thing, he realized, though he couldn't quite see how working for a pasta company could cause it. Perhaps the stress lay more at home? Coping with very young children was never easy, as far as he remembered, though Laura had taken the brunt of it. These days far more was expected of fathers, which was fair enough.

'When are you coming to stay with us, Father?'

The question he had dreaded.

'That's very kind of you, Susan. I'd like to very much.'

Diary pages rustled importantly.

'What about the weekend after next? We're free then. And the bungalow down the road that I told you about is still up for sale. You really should view it. It would be perfect for you.'

Dogs with meaty bones could learn a thing or two from his daughter-in-law.

'I'll certainly bear it in mind.'

'Are you still taking those vitamin pills, Father?'

'Of course.' He'd thrown them out long ago.

'You have to take special care of yourself at your age.'

'I do, I assure you.'

'Regular exercise is very important.'

'Yes, I'm aware of that.'

Walking was about the only exercise that he took these days.

'There's a very good Pilates class near us. I go on a Saturday morning while Marcus takes care of the children. You could come with me and have a go.'

In his day, he had been reasonably competent at unarmed combat.

'I think it might be too much for me.'

'Oh, no. We do a lot of floor work lying on a mat, with tiny movements up and down. Nothing vigorous. It's all about inner corps strength, you see, and getting a strong supple body. It improves flexibility and agility and prevents injury. Ballet dancers use it a lot. And we have a very nice lady teacher.'

'I'm sure.'

'You'll think about it, then? It would do you a lot of good.'

He promised to think and was hoping that the conversation might be drawing to a close when Susan suddenly said, 'Eric wants a word with you.'

'Hallo, Grandfather.'

'Hallo there, Eric. How are you?'

'All right. Are you coming to stay with us soon?'

'That's the general idea.'

'Can we go somewhere? Just you and me?'

With luck, they might be able to slip the leash. 'Where would you like to go?'

'You choose.'

Bovington Tank Museum had been a big success on Eric's visit to Pond Cottage. Something similar was called for now in Norfolk. Manly stuff. Somewhere no woman would want to tread.

He said, 'I'll think about it. See if I can come up with an idea.'

He hung up and did some thinking, though not about the Pilates class, or the bungalow. He thought about entertaining Eric. An old wartime airfield similar to Buckby was a possibility. Norfolk was riddled with them, after all.

He and Eric could track one down together, go into the abandoned control tower, walk down the old runway, explore the ruined buildings. Look for clues to imagine how it had once been. It was definitely a good idea.

He went out into the garden and inspected the border where there were already blowsy signs of autumn. It needed a good tidy-up, he reckoned. Dead flowers snipped off, plants cut back or taken out, plans made for replacements and for next year. He'd ask Naomi if she had any suggestions.

There was no sign of Thursday who would sometimes make a casual appearance and shadow him at a distance. The huff was likely to take some time to get over.

He progressed to the pond where the pet shop fish rose up to greet him. When he sprinkled some of the fish food he had brought with him they darted about, but without the greedy frenzy in The Grange lake, and the water was clear and clean.

There had been something very unpleasant about that blanket weed and he didn't envy Geoffrey the problem. It was horrible to think of Don Wilson floundering and choking in its clutches. He wondered if the ghost carp had been circling, waiting to move in? A totally unnecessary death. Sober he would surely have survived. But, as the police inspector had pointed out, it was very easy to drown when drunk.

He thought about the Australian telling his unbelievable tale of his crew's survival pact: how they'd deliberately tipped the odds in their favour. And he thought about the rest of the crew hustling him away from the dinner. Miss Warner had described the noise made as they had manhandled him up the stairs past her bedroom as quite unnecessary. They had been swearing loudly at their mid-upper gunner, she had said. Not surprising since he had spoilt their evening, but he would not have put them down as men likely to make an unruly commotion in someone else's home. Nor had Miss Warner.

He took the shed key from his pocket and unlocked the door. Inside, it was undisturbed. Everything was re-assuringly in its place. The parts of the Matilda tank were lying on the workbench exactly as he had placed them. He was looking forward to resuming Step Nine where he had left off and assembling the turret. He opened up the Naomi-proof sacking curtains and unfolded the instruction sheet.

And then, for no particular reason, he found himself thinking about Don Wilson again. Drunks, in his experience, usually slept it off. They didn't wake up, get up and go out. They stayed put until they eventually came to, hours later. It was nature's infallible recovery programme.

He remembered that the crew had said that the Australian did crazy things when he was drunk but getting up and going out boating seemed not so much crazy as highly unlikely. There was no question that he had been drinking heavily at the dinner, not to mention previously at the lunch. Enough to require his removal back to The Grange and hauling up the stairs to bed. His tie had been loosened, his watch and shoes taken off, a cover put over him. The crew had done the same for him many times in the past. They had said so.

But what if on this occasion, things had gone differently? What if when they had arrived back at the house, Wilson had insisted on blundering off on his bomber's moon jaunt on the lake and that his crew had run out of patience at that point and left him to it? Washed their hands of him? Abandoned him to his fate? The man had, after all, been telling outrageous and slanderous tales at their expense, even if intended as a joke. They had every reason to be angry and fed up with him. But, in that case, why go through a noisy pretence of taking him upstairs to bed? Of rumpling the bedclothes and denting the pillow? And what was the Australian's watch doing on the bedside table, not on his wrist, and why were his shoes in the bedroom and not on his feet? None of it made sense.

'Hallooo there, Hugh! What are you up to in here?'

Idiot that he was, he had left the shed door slightly ajar. It was now flung open wide and Naomi's bulk, draped in the purple kaftan he remembered from before (but without the panama hat) filled the gap. Before he could block her way she had advanced further, looking around.

'This reminds me of Cecil's hideaway. Full of tools and things he never used.'

It was not the first time he had felt a certain rapport with Naomi's late husband. Nor would it be the last.

'I'm sure he used them.'

'No, I don't think he actually *did* anything. I see you're busy, though.'

She picked up the model box lid from the workbench, examining the picture on the front.

'I used to know someone who served in tanks. He was in the desert in the war with the Eighth. Said it was hell on earth. Unbelievable heat, flies, sandstorms . . . he told some horrific stories.'

He'd heard a few himself – enough to have convinced him that tank crews, like bomber crews, were made up of pretty special men. He removed the lid firmly from Naomi's grasp.

'Time for a drink.'

But she stayed where she was, not to be hurried, examining the pieces on the workbench, fingering them in turn, putting them back in the wrong places.

'I didn't know you were a model maker, Hugh.'

'I'm not. I'm just following instructions. Gluing things together.'

'Well, it all looks very complicated.'

'It isn't, really.'

'What's this piece?'

'Part of the turret.' He returned it to its correct spot. 'Let's go and have that drink.'

Once more, she ignored the suggestion.

'Of course, they're a man thing, aren't they?'

'What are?'

'Sheds. No sane woman would go and lurk all day in a damp old hut at the bottom of the garden, but men love them. I suppose it's to escape.'

She might have a point, he thought grimly.

'Escape?'

'I once read in the newspaper about a man who lived in his shed for a whole year to avoid his creditors.'

'I'm not avoiding creditors, Naomi.'

'Of course you aren't, Hugh. You're not the type at all. You're making models. If you weren't doing that you'd be tinkering with a bike, or something perfectly harmless. Sheds can be quite sinister places, you know. Remember the bit in that famous book about a farm with something nasty in the woodshed? I bet men get up to all sorts of things.'

'I can assure you, Naomi, that *I* don't get up to anything. The only vice in here is the one screwed on to the end of this workbench.'

She cackled loudly at that. 'Oh, Hugh, I was only joking.'

'I'm relieved to hear it.'

It still took some time to manoeuvre her out of the shed and on to the terrace where he fetched the prepared tray and set it on the table. There was no need to enquire about her drink which was always the same – a three-finger slug of neat Chivas Regal with a splash of plain tap water and no ice. His was the same but without the water. He raised his glass.

'Good health, Naomi.'

'Same to you, Hugh.'

The terrace was bathed in warm evening sunlight and it would stay that way for at least another hour or more. He acknowledged his debt to Naomi for insisting that building a sundowner terrace was a good idea, but he would make very sure that in future she stayed out of his shed.

'So, what's been happening while I've been away?'

'Well, the big news is that Ruth is definitely expecting. Next April. She let the cat out of the bag herself.'

'That's very happy news.'

'Yes, isn't it? An heir to the Manor. Someone to keep it in the family and away from all those hedgehog managers.'

'Hedge fund.'

'Whatever they call themselves. Hog suits them better. Can you imagine how they'd wreck it? Swimming pools, jacuzzis and all the rest, with the house done up like in the photos you see in those dreadful interior decorating magazines. They never seem to have anywhere comfortable to sit, have you noticed? And the fireplaces are always miles away.'

There was some truth in that, he thought. The difference between a home and a showcase. You lived in one and showed off in the other.

He watched a blackbird hopping across the grass before it flew up into the lilac tree.

He said, 'Speaking of cats, Thursday's still off somewhere.'

'Don't worry, he'll be back when he thinks you've suffered enough guilt.'

There was probably truth in that as well.

'Well, the fish in the pond are doing all right and the water's stayed clear. Where I was staying they had a bad problem with blanket weed and it was a lake, not a small pond.'

'Dreadful stuff. Almost impossible to get rid of, though I did read about some kind of straw you can float on the water that can do the trick. I'll see if I can find out more for your friend, if you like.'

'He'd be very grateful. What other local news?'

'Well, you know Steve at the garage?'

The burly and tattoo-armed mechanic had done some excellent work on the Riley.

'Yes, what about him?'

'He's let it be known that in future he'd like to be known as Steph.'

'Steph?'

'Short for Stephanie. Apparently it's been brewing up for years. He's not taken to wearing frocks, or anything like that, just a sort of shiny jump suit with earrings and his hair is in a pony tail. Otherwise you wouldn't notice much difference. Marjorie is hoping that the Major won't notice anything at all when he takes their Escort in.'

It was amazing, the Colonel thought, the life that lay beneath the surface of an apparently stagnant pond. He must be sure to remember to address Steve as Steph from now on.

'What else?'

'Well, I ought to warn you that plans are already afoot with the Amateur Dramatic Society for this year's Christmas pantomime.'

'But it's only August.'

'It's never too early as far as they're concerned. Did you see last year's?'

He had been spared by Alison's visit. 'My daughter was staying.'

'They did *Puss in Boots*, if I remember rightly. This time they've decided to write one themselves. Be original.'

'That sounds interesting.'

'No, it doesn't, Hugh. It sounds disastrous. And Marjorie Cuthbertson is to produce, of all people. Apparently she did things with army dramatic societies when she and the Major were serving abroad. Can you imagine?'

'Not easily.'

'Nor me. Well, you have been warned. They'll be trying to rope you in if you don't watch out.'

'Mrs Bentley already tried once. Without success.'

'Flora Bentley and Marjorie Cuthbertson are two different kettles of fish, Hugh. *Méfiez-vous.*'

'Don't worry, I will.'

Naomi downed some more whisky.

'By the way, what about the Australian who drowned in the boating accident?'

'What about him?'

'Well, tell me more.'

'There's nothing much to tell. He got very drunk at the RAF reunion dinner in Lincoln on the Saturday evening and his old crew drove him back to Buckby and put him to bed in his room at the B and B. It seems he must have got up some time during the night, taken the rowing boat out on to the lake and fallen overboard. I found him floating face down in the water next morning.'

'*You* found him?'

'Yes. Why?'

'You're always finding bodies, Hugh. You really must break the habit, you know.'

'It's not a habit, Naomi. I just happened to be there. I don't go around looking for them.'

'And you're certain that it was an accident?'

'I don't see why it would have been anything else. The police were perfectly satisfied. The post-mortem showed he was very drunk and he drowned. He obviously fell overboard – most probably trying to retrieve the oars. The boat was empty nearby with the oars floating on the surface.'

'You said he could swim, didn't you?'

'Yes, but apparently drunks drown very easily.'

'And he was definitely alone?'

'So far as anyone knows. His crew went off to bed after they'd tucked him up. I was at the same dinner with Geoffrey and Heather and when we got back to the house later everyone was asleep with their lights out.'

Naomi squinted at the lowered level in her glass and

hooked out a small insect with her little finger. 'But you don't seem very happy about it, Hugh.'

He frowned. 'He was a strange sort of chap. Rather the odd one out. The rest of the crew had all kept in close touch but he'd gone back to Australia after the war and they hadn't seen or heard of him for years. He doesn't seem to have amounted to very much, in spite of his war service. A bit of a sad case, it struck me. When he won some money on the races he spent it on flying back to England for the reunion. He hadn't told them he was coming, though. It was quite a surprise for them when he turned up at the B and B.'

'A nice surprise?'

'It seemed so. They were together again after more than fifty years. They'd been young men living through a life or death experience together. They'd done a full tour of thirty operations and somehow they'd all survived. That makes for a pretty strong bond.'

'So my Lancaster uncle always said. What was your Australian's place in the crew?'

'He was their mid-upper gunner. And a good one, too, I think. They had no complaints. He drank a lot off duty, but never when flying.'

'How about the rest of his crew? What were they like?'

'Thoroughly decent types. Modest. Unassuming. Unpretentious. You'd never guess what they'd done in the war just by looking at them.'

'You didn't have to try with my uncle. He was a great line-shooter. He told it all.'

'This Australian could certainly tell some stories. He came out with an extraordinary one at the reunion dinner. I didn't hear it myself but someone else told me about it afterwards.'

'What story?'

He hesitated for a moment.

'Come on, spit it out, Hugh. I can see it's bugging you.'

'Well, he claimed that after he and the other six had done their first two operations and found out how bad it was, they agreed between themselves that they would do everything they could to increase their chances of survival.'

'Makes sound sense.'

'In theory, yes, but it wasn't quite so straightforward. He said that they deliberately planned to drop their bombs short of the targets and turn for home as soon as possible.'

'Ah . . .'

'He also said that they decided that if they were given a particularly tough target they'd find something wrong with the plane to give them an excuse to turn back, counting on the next op being easier. Another trick was to simply dump their bombs in the sea.'

'Quite a story!'

'He was drunk, Naomi. It was some kind of sick joke. Those men were the very best. Heroes.'

'They were human beings as well as heroes, Hugh. They can't *all* have been perfect.'

'Well the men I met at the B and B were the genuine article. I'd stake my life on them.'

'Luckily you don't have to. The Australian did, and look what happened to him. Did he say anything else extraordinary?'

He hesitated again.

'He told a local newspaper reporter that he thought serving in Bomber Command was a mug's game. He claimed the RAF didn't care about the huge losses because there were always plenty of other mugs to take their place.'

'Another of his little jokes?'

'It was his opinion, apparently.'

'How about the rest of his crew? Did they share his opinion?'

'Not that I'm aware. They just had the odd grouse, that's all. Nothing unusual.'

'Well, if they *did* all think the same – that they were

being taken for mugs – then you can bet your bottom dollar that what your Aussie said about them faking things was true. And his turning up unexpectedly for the reunion would have been rather an embarrassment to your modest and unassuming crew. They must have been quite worried. He'd been safely twelve thousand miles away for all those years, hopefully dead, and suddenly he wasn't. He was very much alive. There they were, all set to have a lovely nostalgic RAF reunion weekend, a great big fuss being made of them at long last, and all of a sudden their old buddy, who's fond of a drop, starts spilling some very shocking beans. Beans they'd kept secret for years.'

'He made it all up, Naomi.'

'Did he, Hugh? Hasn't it occurred to you that he might have been telling the truth? *In vino veritas*?'

It had, but he had dismissed the idea. His army years had given him experience of all kinds of men. So far as he was concerned, the Lancaster crew were sound; their mid-upper the only questionable link in the chain.

'What exactly are you inferring, Naomi?'

'His crew said they put their chap to bed when they got back from the dinner. Right?'

'Yes. Another guest heard them taking him upstairs.'

'Heard, not saw? Am I right?'

'They made quite a lot of noise, apparently.'

'Noise is easy to make. They could have been faking it. Supposing he wasn't there at all? Supposing he'd already drowned in the lake?'

'You mean he'd taken the boat out and fallen overboard?'

'No. I mean he'd been taken out and pushed over.'

'That's ridiculously far-fetched, Naomi.'

'It's not far-fetched at all. Don't you see? Once he'd started blabbing about what they'd got up to during the war, something had to be done fast before they lost their precious hero status. He had to be got rid of.'

'Do you seriously think that one of them was responsible?'

'Not one of them, Hugh. All of them.'

'*All of them.* For heaven's sake, Naomi!'

'Just like in that Agatha Christie book – the one that took place on the train.'

'I've never read any of Agatha Christie's books.'

'If you had, you'd have twigged what happened. All six of your heroic crew did it. They didn't take their gunner up to bed, like they pretended. Instead, they took him straight to the lake, shoved him in the boat and rowed out to where it was deepest. Then they all heaved him overboard together and whenever he came up for air they took it in turns to push him under again.'

'That's absolutely absurd!'

'No, it isn't. In the Christie book twelve people take turns to stab a drugged man in his train sleeping compartment, one at a time, so they don't know who actually delivered the final *coup de grâce*. That made it easier for them. More acceptable. Exactly the same sort of thing here. When the Aussie finally stopped bobbing up your chaps rowed back to the bank, shoved the boat and the oars out on to the lake and made all that noise going upstairs, so it seemed that he was with them.'

'His shoes were found up in the bedroom. So was his watch. How do you explain that?'

'Easy. They took them off him in the boat and put them up there to corroborate their story.'

'The shoes I could understand. But why the watch?'

'You're losing your touch, Hugh. It was a cheap watch, right?'

'It certainly looked it. Very cheap.'

'If it had been expensive it would have gone on working in the water. You know what they always say in the classy ads about them being waterproof to a hundred feet or something. Though I can never see why that matters. I mean, who's going to go deep sea diving with a gold Omega strapped to their wrist? The point is, being so cheap, his watch would probably have stopped the minute they tipped him in, which would have given away the exact time of death. They couldn't risk that, could they? He was supposed to have drowned much later, during the night when everyone was asleep. So they took it off – along with the shoes.'

The watch had been positioned carefully on its side on the table. But now that he thought more about it, there had been no need for such consideration, and no precedent from the old wartime days. Wilson waking up, fully clothed, from a drunken sleep would have looked for the time on his wrist, not on a bedside table. Crew huts would not have had such luxurious refinements. Only lockers.

Naomi had drained her glass. He knew his cue.

'The other half?'

'I don't mind if I do.'

He got up to do the refills, making them both a bit stiffer than usual. Four fingers at least. When he sat down again, he said, 'You've got quite an imagination, Naomi. You make it sound almost plausible.'

'Well, it is, isn't it?'

'He could have got up during the night and gone out boating on his own, as everybody, including the police, thought must have happened. That's very plausible too.'

'When my Lancaster uncle went on a bender in his youth, which was every time he came back on leave, he'd be out for the count for at least ten hours. My mother let him sleep it off and cooked him kippers for breakfast.'

'Maybe Australians have harder heads.'

'Come on, Hugh! That won't wash. He was a tired old man who'd drunk far too much as usual. It would have taken him all night to recover. The rest of the crew must have planned what they were going to do when they were carting him back after the dinner, drunk as a skunk in a back seat. Six against one. Easy. They didn't want to stop being brave war heroes, did they? Or have to give back their medals?'

He said slowly, 'Actually, I don't think they had any medals. At any rate, they weren't wearing them for the church service.'

'Isn't that unusual after a full tour? Surely, the skipper, at least, generally got something? All my uncle's crew got a gong. But, of course, if your lot kept turning back and their bombing wasn't so hot, maybe that's the reason. Didn't the Aussie say anything to you? People usually unburden themselves to you, don't they?'

'We didn't talk much. I do remember him saying that they could have killed a whole lot more Germans, if they'd wanted to. That they didn't drop nearly enough bombs. It seemed an odd thing to say.'

'There you are, then.'

'No, I'm not, Naomi. I'm not anywhere. He wasn't necessarily referring to any cowardice. And it's certainly no proof that his crew drowned him to stop him talking.'

She shrugged. 'Have it your own way, Hugh. But you're letting them get away with it, if you don't do anything.'

'There was a fully competent police inspector in charge and he was satisfied that it was an accident. There was also a post-mortem.'

'But *you're* not satisfied, are you?'

He fingered his glass. 'I don't know what to think, Naomi, to be honest.'

'In the Christie book, the victim was a very evil man who had kidnapped and murdered a child and had never been caught. The twelve people were self-appointed executioners, who had all known the child and wanted to avenge its death. The same number as a jury, you see.'

'What happened in the end?'

'Hercule Poirot, the detective, solved it, as usual – I suppose you've heard of him?'

'Of course I have.'

'Well, he decided that justice had been done and he retired from the case.'

'So, they got away with it?'

'Yes. But it's rather different with your six chaps, isn't it? They weren't administering justice, they were saving their precious faces and reputations. They were all seven in it together with the plan to save their skins in the war and those six were in it together when it came to getting rid of their mid-upper gunner at the reunion.

We were all in it together. Now that he thought about it, the skipper's remark to him had been open to a very different interpretation.

'Only in your very vivid imagination, Naomi.'

She waved her hand indifferently. 'I've told you what happened, Hugh. You must do as you please.'

'To change the subject,' he said after a moment's strained silence, 'Do you have any suggestions for my border? I think it needs some improvement.'

'Echinops bannaticus. They'd look good at the back – fill in that blank you've got there. Ruth has got some. And I'd get rid of the meconopsis, if I were you. It's not looking at all happy. Get something else that will be. And you could go in for some of the wild self-seeders and stick them around. Forget-me-nots, poppies, ox-eye daisies, cow parsley would all come up through the other plants so you get a nice natural, meadowy look. Very Highgrove. You have to be ruthless with the cow parsley, though or it will take over. The trick is to cut it down before it seeds.'

He had long admired the naturalness of Naomi's own garden where practically everything seemed to have seeded itself, but rather doubted he would ever be able to create the same effect.

'Any more ideas?'

'Well, you could try some verbena. "Lavender Spires", say. Very well behaved and a good link plant.'

They went on discussing the herbaceous border until the

second halves were finished and Naomi took her leave. The subject of Don Wilson had not been raised again but, as he opened the front door for her, he said, 'Have you read many detective books, Naomi?'

'I used to read loads. Don't seem to get the time now.'

'Did you always guess whodunnit?'

'Oh, yes. Never failed. On the button every time.'

FOURTEEN

He took another tour of the garden, hoping as he did so, that Thursday might turn up, but there was no sign of him. Back indoors, he opened a tin of sardines in oil, tipped the contents into the cat's bowl, marked DOG, and mashed the fish up for easy eating. Mrs Moffat had mentioned pilchards, which were essentially the same thing, and this particular brand, which he sometimes ate on toast himself, was very good. The bowl was kept near the open door. If Thursday's sense of smell was still any good, they would be a powerful attraction.

He went into the sitting room, sat down in his wing back chair and picked up the phone. When he dialled the Cheetham's number, Geoffrey answered. He told him about Naomi's tip for the blanket weed.

'Apparently, there's some kind of special straw you can get that works well. She's going to find out more about it and I'll let you know.'

'Thanks, Hugh. I'll try anything.'

'How is Heather?'

'Rallying, I'm glad to say. We've been talking about the B and B and I've persuaded her that we should carry on. In fact, we're going to do up another of the attic rooms. She's even agreed to keep the boat.'

'So, the police haven't been bothering you again?'

'Bothering us? Why would they?'

'I just wondered if there had been any more developments about Don Wilson's death.'

'None at all. It's all finished and done with. Everyone in the village has been very supportive.'

Supportive was another key word these days; like stress.

If the Cheethams had the village on their side, the accidental death of a passing stranger was unlikely to cause any long-term problems. It would be forgotten very quickly.'

He said, 'Did the inspector ever happen to mention how long they reckoned Wilson had been dead before I found him?'

'No. And I never asked. Why?'

'I was just curious.'

'Well, we can get on with our lives now, thank God. I'm looking forward to getting started on that control tower museum project that I told you about. I think we can make it happen.'

'I'm sure you can.'

'We must keep busy at our stage in life, Hugh – don't you agree?'

'Certainly.'

He thought of keeping-busy activities he had lined up at the moment. Driving the community minibus once a week, clearing footpaths once a month, cutting the churchyard grass when it needed it. Various other noble deeds and now the distant spectre of the village Christmas pantomime. His old friend was to be envied with his museum.

He said, 'I'll let you know about the straw.'

'Thanks. I appreciate it. And come and see us again soon, Hugh. We'll try to make it a quieter stay.'

The cottage was silent. The same silence that he had found intolerable after Laura had died, only broken by the metronomic ticking of the grandfather clock. All his life there had been other people around – family, school friends, fellow officers, Laura, the children – never this devastating silence. Thursday made almost no noise except for occasionally purring gracious approval, but he was there. According to his daily routine, the old cat should have been curled up asleep at the end of the sofa; instead the sofa was empty, its cushions undisturbed. In desperation, the Colonel went through his stack of Gilbert and Sullivan records – the very old-fashioned kind that he had stubbornly kept since he had started collecting them in his school days. He could, he knew, have sat without stirring from his chair and listened to every one of the operettas through headphones clamped to his ears, but it seemed to him that modern recordings lacked substance and depth. Something had been lost in the process: something intrinsic between the listener and the music. It was satisfying – to him at least – to handle a record. To take it from its sleeve, to place it on the turntable, to press the switch and watch the mechanical action begin, before sitting down in his wing-backed chair, whisky in hand, to listen.

> We sail the ocean blue,
> And our saucy ship's a beauty;
> We're sober men and true,
> And attentive to our duty.

The jaunty, salty tune would normally have raised his spirits, but instead he found himself depressed.

Naomi had been right. He wasn't satisfied that Don Wilson's death had been an accident. It had looked like one and the police had concluded that it was one. However, as Naomi had pointed out, if the Australian's tale had had any truth in it he would have been a serious threat to the crew's hero status when he started spilling those beans at the reunion. Someone, as Geoffrey had remarked, might have believed him.

Except that her colourful version of what had happened was guesswork based entirely on a fictional detective story, so far as he could see. He could hardly phone up Inspector Dryden on the strength of it. There was no proof – only his own irrational doubt and Naomi's fertile imagination. Put together, they added up to precisely nothing. And the shoes and the watch were hardly conclusive evidence. It was true that some of the crew seemed to have harboured a few minor grievances – but so did most servicemen, in his experience. Authority was there to be grumbled about.

In the Agatha Christie book, the killers had got away with it, though apparently for an acceptable reason. The victim had been an evil villain, the perpetrators of his death fully justified in killing him, and the great Hercule Poirot had diplomatically chosen to retire from the case.

The Colonel had no case to retire from. The police would not be interested in his totally unfounded suspicions or Naomi's wild speculations. Geoffrey and Heather were now happily getting on with their lives. Don Wilson was dead and honourably buried. The only people who knew the truth, or would ever know it, were the six remaining members of the Lancaster crew.

> *When at anchor we ride*
> *On the Portsmouth tide,*
> *We have plenty of time to play.*
>
> *Ahoy! Ahoy!*
> *The balls whistle free.*
> *Ahoy! Ahoy!*
> *Over the bright blue sea,*
> *We stand to our guns, to our guns all day.*

For all he knew, the Lancaster crew had stood to their guns all night, and done everything they were supposed to do. For all he knew they were heroes, not cowards at all. Who was he to question it?

He let the record finish and turn itself off. When he checked in the kitchen, the bowl of mashed sardines remained untouched. The fridge contained two eggs, some milk and a bit of Cheddar cheese. Ingredients for an omelette that he couldn't be bothered to make. Back in the sitting room, he sat down again in the wing chair and picked up his whisky glass. The silence was back, except for the relentless ticking of the grandfather clock.

Freda Butler was making her customary end-of-the-day sweep with the U-boat captain's binoculars, somehow acquired by her late father, the Admiral. She stood at her sitting-room window traversing the village green, much as the original owner would have deployed them across the ocean from his conning tower.

There wasn't a great deal of interest going on, it had to be said. Nice Dr Harvey had driven by in his grey Renault on his way home to the Manor. How romantic it had been that he and dear Ruth had married and what happy news it was about the coming baby. So satisfactory that new life was being breathed into the old Manor. She must start knitting at once. A matinee jacket, perhaps? The problem was should it be pink or blue? Nowadays, so she had heard, it was possible to tell if it was a boy or girl, though, of course, she would never dream of asking.

Mrs Cuthbertson had also driven past earlier, crouched over the wheel of the Escort, returning from her ladies' bridge. She had narrowly missed the gatepost turning in to Shangri-La; sometimes she actually hit it.

Miss Butler had also observed Naomi Grimshaw coming out of the Colonel's cottage on the opposite side of the green and returning to Pear Tree Cottage next door. They would have been having their usual evening drink – no doubt out on the Colonel's new terrace in the warm summer weather. Of course, there was no question of any kind of involvement in their case. The dear Colonel had obviously been very much in love with his late wife and was a perfect gentleman, not to mention that Mrs Grimshaw was rather past her best. If, indeed, she had ever had one.

Miss Butler swept the green once more, like the U-boat commander in search of fresh quarry. It soon came into view in the shape of Major Cuthbertson weaving an unsteady

homeward path across the green from the general direction
of the Dog and Duck. Nothing new about that, either. Really,
it was a disgrace how much he drank, though being married
to Mrs Cuthbertson perhaps had its trials and tribulations?
One should never sit in judgement. Most marriages, she had
long ago realized, had their disadvantages and sometimes
she was rather glad that she had remained single. She watched
him veer into the entrance of Shangri-La, missing the gatepost by about the same narrow margin as his wife in the
Escort. Marjorie Cuthbertson would be concocting some
inedible dish in the kitchen and the Major, she knew, would
sneak to the drinks cabinet presented by his old regiment
which unfortunately, and very audibly, played 'Drink to Me
only with Thine Eyes' the moment he opened the lid.

The light was fading and she could see that the Colonel
had switched on the lamp in his sitting room; it was glim-
mering through the windows. He must get very lonely sometimes, just as she did. They had both served in the forces
and had known service camaraderie. Retirement took some
getting used to and the Colonel, naturally, would miss his
wife. As the village knew, he had been away for a few days,
staying with friends in Lincolnshire, but now he was back
on his own again.

Miss Butler shifted the powerful glasses a degree to the
left and picked up a dark shape slipping through the front
gateway to Pond Cottage. Thursday! The ungrateful, bad-
tempered, flea-bitten stray that the Colonel had been kind
enough to give a home. Personally, she would never have
allowed him over the threshold. And the word was that he
had been accommodated at considerable expense in Cat
Heaven during the Colonel's absence.

She kept the binoculars focused on the cat as he trotted
up the pathway and disappeared round the corner, clearly
heading for the back door and the comforts of Pond Cottage.
Cats weren't fools. They knew when they were on to a good
thing.

Miss Butler lowered the heavy binoculars for a moment, picturing the Colonel sitting alone in his armchair. On second thoughts, even a mangy old moggie might be some company. Perhaps Thursday had his uses after all.